The Witching Hours Lullaby

The Witching Hours Lullaby

Shannon Gill Burnett

iUniverse®

THE WITCHING HOURS LULLABY

iUniverse books may be ordered through booksellers or by contacting:

iUniverse
1663 Liberty Drive
Bloomington, IN 47403
www.iuniverse.com
844-349-9409

Because of the dynamic nature of the Internet, any web addresses or links contained in this book may have changed since publication and may no longer be valid. The views expressed in this work are solely those of the author and do not necessarily reflect the views of the publisher, and the publisher hereby disclaims any responsibility for them.

Any people depicted in stock imagery provided by Getty Images are models, and such images are being used for illustrative purposes only.
Certain stock imagery © Getty Images.

ISBN: 978-1-6632-6559-3 (sc)
ISBN: 978-1-6632-6560-9 (e)

Library of Congress Control Number: 2024915789

Print information available on the last page.

iUniverse rev. date: 08/14/2024

Dedicated to my sister; then, now, and always.

ABOUT THE AUTHOR

Shannon Gill Burnett is a native Washingtonian but calls New York her real home for that is where her heart is.

Her first book In the Medium was published in 2012. Ms. Burnett has written seven novels and continues to write daily. The Witching Hours Lullaby is her second novel to be published.

In her off time, she enjoys traveling, exercising, reading and her family. She is a Baltimore Orioles, Washington Nationals and New York Knicks fan.

DISCLAIMER

This storyline and its characters and places are fictious and of the author's imagination only.

No one part of this or the book as whole represents any real person, place, or thing.

The purpose of this book is for entertainment purposes only.

The author concedes all responsibility.

You can't win
If you don't loose

You can't be good
If you can't be true

Determined essence freely abound
You are here and have been found

Textured and woven in the bowels of it all
Fighting for breath, before you fall

Exhausted before rest
Run to the end to give your best

You did it, you won
You are greater than your parts, you are the sum

No one can take it from you, no one will try
A winner's spirit floats into the sky

Launched with the freedom of saying goodbye
You will not falter if you try

A hollow shell is all that's left
I aborted her when we first met

A twisted panic is adorned
My life abandon is forlorn

Caged no more, silence is key
Because that hollow shell set me free

The truth will set you free

Anna

BEFORE
Anna

To know my story and understand its substance, you must understand Oxycontin and the affects it can have on women especially in women over fifty. For me, the time after my knee surgery was euphoric and mysterious and the Oxycontin transported me into a thick haze of suspension, somewhere between the truth and lies, knowing and not knowing; good and bad. Unsure of who I even was, a very slippery slope to maneuver.

When I mixed the Oxycontin with sleeping pills or alcohol, it deepened the mystery and fog within me, not necessarily knowing what was true or false, but maybe, just maybe, that is where this story begins. Understanding that not all accounts of life are so simple, caught between the light and darkness or maybe in the subconscious where we can receive information that helps to understand the mysteries in life. With this information maybe we can help figure out things, or even during heavy premonition, understand the truth. In premonition things come to you so clearly, how can they be false? Maybe premonition is laid upon us to receive the information and then we are left to draw its conclusion, be our own detective.

Simplicity is key, but sometimes things are not so simple, and we need help to get to simplicity, which holds the answers. How can we do that? By paying attention to the cues, trusting ourselves and paying attention to light.

After my knee accident and orthoscopic surgery, I went through something and that something starts here, in my story which becomes their story, a never-ending quest for all that is right, during all that is wrong. Finagling through the muck----searching for it, your truth.

Maybe I was even chosen to have my meniscus tear that day on the court at Holly Oaks Country Club on the tennis court, maybe I was chosen to solve these clues that came to me during the time of recuperation while I was on Oxycontin.

That is how, after all, matters get solved. Someone is chosen to solve the riddles and pillage for the answers to solve even the most painful of stories, deep inside, not ever betrayed, wrapped up in the middle of other people's stories.

Blinded by curiosity and compelled to preserve.

OXYCONTIN

The simplest way to understand OxyContin is as an opioid drug like heroin or opium. It is derived from the same source and has the same basic effects as these illicit substances. Opioids are widely used in medicine because they are among the most efficient pain relievers. Many people meet drugs such as Vicodin, Percocet, and OxyContin through legitimate means. The main defining feature of OxyContin is that it has a time-release formula, the affects lasting for about 12 hours. Percocet releases all the substance at once and lasts only about five hours.

Addiction is the most evident effect of long-term OxyContin abuse on the brain. The brain is initially overwhelmed when the drug signals the extended release of dopamine, unable to continue its normal functioning because of the intense chemical injection. To account for this, as the drug is taken more regularly, the brain adjusts its natural processes, so it isn't overwhelmed anymore. By reducing the number of opiate receptors and producing less dopamine naturally, the brain effectively dampens the effect OxyContin has. This means that the user must take more of the drug to achieve the same effect, and that without the drug, he or she will have a deficit in some neurotransmitters. This effect creates addiction, because the brain has essentially rewired itself to account for the continued presence of the substance. Without it, the individual experiences a wide range of unpleasant side effects, known as withdrawal. The longer the individual takes the drug and the more that is consumed, the more the brain adapts, and the individual becomes addicted. Although using OxyContin more than prescribed commonly leads to addiction, it can also develop from the suggested course of medication.

Many of the long-term effects of the drug come to the forefront during this withdrawal period. Withdrawal usually creates the opposite effect of the drug, so if a woman goes without OxyContin for the first time after months of abuse, she will experience severe pain, depression, and flu-like symptoms such as loss of appetite, runny nose, and sneezing. Irritability and mood swings are also common. Because of these effects, the cravings for another dose of the drug can be intense. One of the main risks of any opioid drug is respiratory depression (or slowed breathing). This is because the drugs depress the central nervous system, which is responsible for breathing. The risk of this is greater in long-term users, those who take more of the drug than prescribed, and anybody who combines it with alcohol.

How does OxyContin affect sleep?

One problem opioids can cause is problems with sleep. They can create problems with sleep quality, falling asleep or conditions like sleep apnea. When your sleep is disrupted, you can experience various complications, such as mood swings, stress, memory problems and an overall reduction in the quality of life.

Can oxycodone cause weird dreams? The use of sustained or strong prescription opioids can cause people, especially those over 50, to hallucinate, have fake premonitions or even dangerous dreams. Using a lower dose or switching to a different opioid may ease these side effects. Talk to your doctor about what you can do to help with bad dreams or hallucinations if you have them.

How do opioids affect women? Long-term use of prescription opioid medications in women can cause hormonal changes, depression and even infertility. Changes in your hormones may affect your period and libido.

What is a premonition in your sleep? Precognitive dreams are the most widely reported occurrences of precognition. Usually, a dream or vision can only be identified as precognitive after the putative event has taken place. When such an event occurs after a dream, it is said to have "broken the dream". "Joseph's Dream", a painting by Rembrandt.

It's no surprise you might have a few vivid dreams or unsettling dreams in your life. You may even be among the 17.8% to 38% of people who have experienced at least one precognitive or premonition dream. These are dreams that seemingly predict the future.

What are visions before going to sleep? They're common and usually not a cause for concern. Up to 70% of people experience them at least once. A hallucination is a false perception of objects or events involving your senses: sight, sound, smell, touch, and taste.

Is intuition the same as premonition? Intuition is the ability to understand something without fully must have all the facts where a premonition is the feeling that something is about to happen. An intuitive person relies on his life and work experiences to guide him. Only a few of us are naturally intuitive in the psyche. Was it fate, was it hallucinations, was it premonition or was it the Oxy?

Finally, there is a risk of severe psychological disturbances in people who abuse OxyContin. In long-term users, hallucinations, delusions, and delirium have all been reported, in addition to mood swings and panic attacks. This doesn't occur in all cases, but is often worse during withdrawal, when many users feel confused or disoriented. Memory issues or even amnesia can develop in long-term abusers, nearly fatal when mixed with alcohol. Oxycontin was in me, but was I part of it? Was I even me, could I even be trusted with all this information that kept coming to me? How else can I explain the dreams, the nightmares, the panic, the proof? Or was I just simply chosen?

Hold fast to dreams because when dreams go
Life is a barren field frozen with snow

PREFACE

....

I am Anna Katherine Davis; complicated wreck, vanquished and defeated, but damn good at keeping face. You must have a poker face to survive here, and I am a natural born survivor. I am a fake until you make a kind of lady, a wanna be nouveau riche, I rub elbows with them all day at the Country club where I work, and when you spend that kind of time with people you just blend in with them. Your comingling fades to lavender from purple and then you are all just the same, accepted, and stupid---- oblivious to anyone else except those who live in your inner sanctum circle. It is all a mystifying cloud of mendacity magnified by haute couture and endless glasses of wine, infidelity and who's who.

I am fifty-year old, divorced, mother of two adult children, and a kick-ass tennis player living in Farmington Connecticut. Holly Oaks to be exact, where the rich of Farmington come to live, and Farmington is already rich so if you live here, you are elite and of good gentry, best in class.

I have been playing tennis since I was eight years old. I was a prodigy then, (with too many to count trophies and ribbons, plaques, and metals), and a semi pro now. This was my path and my parents groomed me for it, this life I have. My father was a pro tennis player in Portugal and my mother wasn't bad with a racquet either. They opened a tennis academy in Connecticut when my father retired at the ripe old age of forty-two. when I was six years old, and my brother was ten. We were forced to learn the game and practice every day. Hating became acceptance and acceptance finally turned into love, love of the game. Tennis was in my framework, my DNA.

I have been in five Grand Slam tournaments (supervised by the International

Tennis Federation (ITF)), and two times in the ATP Tour 250 series, and the Davis Cup (organized by the ITF). A pro's pro I was! Always athletic, the life of being a tennis player demanded nothing less. I ran five miles three times a week, did Yoga and Pilates and indulged in a shiatsu massage weekly.

I played tennis every day and made my living teaching at the Holly Oaks Country Club. I made a mere 85K a year but made it doing what I love. I had enough to live on, being divorced, I was still collecting 500.00 a month in alimony and that combined with my salary provided me enough to buy a townhouse/condo here in Holly Oaks, at the rip off price of 500K. Of course, as an employee of Holly Oaks, my association and club fees were waived and I had all access to all of the amenities. I wasn't rich but presented rich. I always had the ability; never let them know who you really are! I leased a bright red BMW 325i, had a nice home with nice furnishings, ran with the it crowd of Holly Oaks, eating out, drinking, wine tastings, traveling to the Hamptons and West Coast and I could still pay my bills on time. Prada this and Prada that, gold bar chains always adorned my collarbone, and don't think I didn't run up bills at Noelle's Salon on hair, nails, and waxes.

I had many men too, young men, old men, hot men, not so hot men. I was never bored and kept those men in check and balance. Working at the Club and being part of the Country Club life gave me a plethora of endless possibilities. I craved sex more now at fifty, then I did at any other time in my life and had plenty of it. My last boyfriend was a mere twenty-four years old; I met him here at the club at the bar one night at closing, well…. One thing lead to another and let's just say, he became my live-in boyfriend for about six months until he robbed me one night. He left with two hundred dollars in cash, a visa credit card I immediately cancelled and my dead grandmother's pearls and diamond ring. In the end I wasn't even mad about. I felt like maybe that was my price to pay for being a fifty-year-old woman fucking a twenty-four-year-old man, everything has its price, and he was worth it. He could make love, have an orgasm and be back on it in twenty minutes, he wore me out, but truth be told I needed to be ridden.

I was 50 yes, but gorgeous and fit. The Pilates and tennis helped me keep toned and taunt, I could almost pass for 40 if you didn't know me. I thought I was hot shit, I loved me!

I kept myself up too, you could almost be ugly, but if you have access to money and the proper grooming station you could become pretty very quickly, even beautiful. Add to that the right clothes, make up and jewelry combined with the who's who of the Country Club and you were almost movie star material, everyone wanted you! I have a busy career and I am the tennis pro everyone wants to work with. This was it for me, everything aligning at the right time, it was Anna time.

It is the height of tennis lesson season here at the club, mid-summer. Getting kids ready for fall sports and well, let's face it, everyone wants to play tennis in the summer. I have four sessions today; a beginner, two intermediates and a teenage girl who thinks she is Serena. Her parents of course indulge her and convince her that she is good enough to be a Serena, but I know better. I allow them to pay me and I am glad to train her, I can only make her better after all. Maybe that is just the point, sometimes better is good enough.

Young Sara Rainer- the next Serena Williams

Her name is Sara Rainer and she is on time today, donned in her Izod Lacoste mini tennis skirt and matching top with a 75.00 Sofibella matching black visor, she came to play, like always. Completely entitled would not do this teenager going on forty justice, as she is truly a force in the making. She even tells her parents how things are going to be and sometimes even treats them like her children. Beckoning orders and barking demand, not so indifferent for an only child and a tennis prodigy. Born rich and talented, she gets her way all the time!

Sara had been to the State Championship with her school team as a sophomore already, combining experience with her talent. Sara and her family live in Allen Oak, a suburb of Farmington for the affluent and old money, no nouveau riche here. Most of these residents were pedigreed and went to the Ivy's, Dartmouth, Yale, Princeton and even Harvard, and the Rainer's fit right in. Her parents were already preparing Sara in every way for Dartmouth, their chosen alma mater. Oh, and she would be accepted, two legacies and Sara's resume, not even a question.

It was hot today and I had been warming up and hitting a few balls with the groundskeeper Eddie, we played tennis together a lot, Eddie was someone I trusted and over time had come to value as a friend. It was a surprising friendship, me----all County Club and posh and Eddie whose parents were migrants from Cuba, dirt poor and uneducated. Eddie's parents left Cuba when Eddie was just eight years old in 1976 after the Proclamation new Cuban Socialist Constitution and Castro's being elected and from what Eddie tells me, his father died along the exile. He does not speak of it much, not even to me, even when I ask. Our friendship survives on that, that trust.

At that time there was so much political disillusionment and uncertainty, Eddie's parents wanted a more secure and healthy future, which is why they exiled. They left everything they had and fled to the United Sates with their beloved son. His mom never got a break here though, or their slice of American Pie. No, his mother simply worked their fingers to the bone, and died an early death. Not the so American Dream they sought after when fleeing their motherland.

This hurt Eddie, and I think stopped him dead in his tracks, America had not been the faithful friend he looked for, but rather, he burned in effigy over his parents and never really moved forward. Eddie has been at the Club his whole adult life thirty-four years total and still has so much more to give even at fifty-four, I don't think he plans on retiring anytime soon, truth be known, Eddie has nowhere else to go and will probably dig his own grave underneath these lush grounds before he dies, in the dirt and soil loyal to his crepe myrtle trees.

Eddie and I meet somewhere though when we spent our time together. Two wanton hearts, looking for the end of the rainbow, where life imitates art and art imitates sadness. We had a real meeting of minds; he was maybe even my one true friend.

We were almost done with our set when she approached the court.

"Hi Sara," I say. "Eddie is leaving and I am warmed up, we are going to work on your back hand and serve today." "Great," she says. "I am trying out for the Varsity team next month and Coach says my back hand is weak and I need to focus on that." "My parents need to see marked improvement." "Grab your racquet, let's see what you got," I say.

Her backhand was ok, but not at a place where she would make the Varsity Team or please her judgmental parents. The back hand is my specialty and I have devised and implemented some key points and focus to make anyone's back hand better. This core strategy is what makes me a great tennis instructor. "Sara, let's work on some of the basics now." I have executed a list as a tennis coach I think works for all of my students and with any tennis player in fact.

Making contact with the ball: Try to make contact with the ball when it is not directly in front of you. If you are right-handed, you should make contact a little off to your left side. The ball should be a little bit in front of you. You should be in a similar position as you would be when turning a doorknob.

Racquet-face control: Beginners often struggle with racquet-face control and then lose control of the ball. It is very important to be mindful of how you hold the racquet and how that changes the directions the strings face because wherever your racquet face is pointing the moment that you make contact with the ball, that is where the ball is going to go. When you are just starting out, the goal should be to get the ball in play. As you get a little better, try to get it in but in the direction, you are aiming for. Focus on controlling your racquet face and where it is pointing the moment you make contact with the ball.

Grip: People can hold a racquet in many ways. In terms of the backhand, this includes hitting a two-handed backhand or a one-handed backhand. And while the two-handed backhand – where the dominant hand is at the bottom of the handle, with the non-dominant hand on top – is more common in today's game, the most important thing is to use the grip you are most comfortable with and which gives you the most control.

Ultimately, the way you hold the grip translates to how the racquet face is pointing, so it really doesn't matter which grip you use as long as you are able to control the racquet face. In terms of holding on to a racquet, it's important that you aren't trying to choke the life out of it. In terms of a scale from 1 to 10, if 10 is the absolute tightest you can grip the racquet, you want your grip to be at about a 3.

Swing: The harder you swing, the farther the ball is going to go. The most important thing is to be able to keep the ball on the court when you are a beginner, so keeping your backhand swing at a level that you're able to keep the ball on the court is your No. 1 priority.

Footwork: In general, try to be as light on your feet as possible.

"Let's try and hit some balls and focus on your back hand swing now." "Ok Ms. Davis, I am ready." After our lengthy warm up and going over the basics of the back hand we start to hit some balls.

Back and forth, back, and forth hitting the ball, she, and I with such vigor. Two ladies burning up the court, with their love of this game. Our hearts mutually lock over a racquet and a ball, our spirits soar together high in this impossible moment.

She is doing well, hitting the ball with precision and a form back hand, yes, she is getting it now. I can see her face in that Tennis Club picture taken at high school. She is getting it, she is getting there!

The she hits one so hard I think I will miss the ball, when I dive and lunge at that same time with my whole body's force and momentum carrying through the shot, when my knee doesn't quite make it. I hear something like a rubber band snap in my knee. I collapsed in pain and watch the little yellow tennis ball go out of play.

I can't think the pain is so bad, I am in total agony. My whole leg is on fire, and it feels like the sharpest ax has gone through my right knee cap. The sunlight blurs and my head is spinning until I hear Eddie, "Anna, Anna?"

I am taken to Holly Oaks Hospital by Eddie and I awaiting my MRI when my best friend and accomplice walks through the double doors of the hospital and pulls back my triage curtain open. Her name is Lauren Bates, and she is a force of nature, a force majeure! "What the fuck have done to yourself Anna?" "We have plans tonight remember, the Bridges Event for colon cancer at the Club, don't you remember." "You bought the new Ann Taylor Cocktail Dress; I am giving a speech." "Oh well, they will have to do without me Laur, I am a bit tied up at the moment." Eddie says goodbye and ducks out, "I will call you later," he says.

The doctor walks in, my right medial meniscus is severed.

She explains a torn meniscus can result from any activity that causes you to forcefully twist or rotate your knee, such as aggressive pivoting or sudden stops and turns, like teaching and playing tennis. Even kneeling, deep squatting or lifting something heavy can sometimes lead to a torn meniscus. In older adults, degenerative changes of the knee can contribute to a torn meniscus with little or no trauma, just a misstep.

I will be in a soft cast for about a week and face arthroscopic surgery. The pain is unbearable and my leg cannot bear weight so I am on crutches too. The doctor has prescribed me 10mg of Oxycontin to be taken every 12 hours for the pain. Other than that, I am free to go and can call and schedule my surgery tomorrow.

This old tennis pro is going to have about two months off from work to deal with my knee, surgery, and my recovering. After that, I can hopefully ease back into tennis.

Lauren stayed with me the whole time I was in the hospital and missed the event. She was high maintenance, but a great friend.

I had already taken a dose of Oxy in the hospital and won't be due until morning, but she stopped and filled my prescription anyway then stopped at a Boston Market and ordered 50.00 worth of food, she said she wanted me to have some supplies in the house, she even ordered an entire apple pie. "Jesus, Lauren," I say, "who is going to eat all of this food?" She just swishes my hand away like one of my tennis backhands.

Once home, Lauren helped me get in the front door and into bed. She helped me get undressed and comfortable in my favorite short night shirt. "Here is some bottled water and your meds, I am going to make you a plate of food," she said. "I am not hungry Lauren, I am so tired, I want to go to sleep." "Can you just lock the door behind you when you leave?" "Are you sure?" she asks, I nod.

When I hear the door lock and her car pull off, I get a bit restless, and decide to take one more Oxycontin even though I am not due for seven hours, what can it hurt? I swallow the little pill and lay back on my pillow, I begin to drift.

I am somewhere between a lullaby and a dream when everything turns to black. I wake up in a panic and sweat almost forgetting I have a fucked-up knee as jump out of bed. I just had the worst nightmare ever, but it seemed so real. I can just remember parts of it now, fragments really. Those fragments were terrifying and chilling, they were in my bones. The vision dissipates, but I can remember every detail. Like Monet's work, abstract, but if you get close enough it makes perfect sense.

Somebody is dead or going to die soon. Bloody mess, bloody mess. He is going to kill you, kill you all! Blood splattered grounds, holy sites where these girls are murdered in and out of my consciousness.

My fleeting thoughts and throbbing head erase any rational thought as I crawl back into my warm bed.

Those poor girls, I have to help them.

Surgery

BRING ME ALL OF YOUR DREAMS,
You DREAMER,
BRING ME ALL YOUR
HEART MELODIES

THAT I MAY WRAP THEM
IN A BLUE CLOUD- CLOTH
AWAY FROM THE TOO-ROUGH
FINGERS
OF THE WORLD

The fingers on the hand that wants to hurt you
And devour you like sugar sop

A child's dream gone forever
Once you let the Devil drop

Oxytocin is known to modulate reactivity of the amygdala to social emotions and the amygdala, in turn, is modulated by REM sleep. Despite the multiple ways in which oxytocin may influence sleep and dreams, no study, as far as I know, has directly examined the effects of oxytocin administration on sleep and dreams. A mystery to many, a reality to some. Not having a firm understanding of dreams anyhow as humans, and an understanding of what we dream in large, if it is real or not, eschewed with a medication or alcohol can be perceived as real or false with no way to real prove either case. I never understood any of this until it started happening to me.

My surgery has come and gone and is now over. It feels like I slid into a warm bath of bubbly ooze watching my body float onto the operating table and then turn to black. I awaken on what feels like a rock-hard slab, with no give, stiff, like a corpse. I awaken to see blurred lights beckoning me home like a warm shadow lending a hug. The lights are brighter and brighter pulling me in towards them. A euphoric bliss about me, like being trapped inside of bubble ready to burst. My eyelids flutter, and I have a pasty taste inside of mouth like glue, I am thirsty, I think I open my eyes, I think I hear voices; I start to come to.

Then I do hear a familiar voice, sweet and tempered not speaking directly to me, but around me. I think, I know, it is my Lauren.

My eyelids are so heavy but needing to open. I look down at myself on the slab and can only see one leg, Oh My God, I think, the cut it off, but at closer examination I can see my right leg wrapped in a beige Ace Bandage from the top of my thigh to below my knee. Yes, as I came to, I realize I have just had arthroscopic surgery to repair my torn meniscus.

"The doctor will be into to see you shortly," says the nurse. "You are in the recovering room and your friend is in the lobby; may I bring in her now to be with you?" "She has been asking to be with you." "Yes," I manage to say with all of my might.

Moments later Lauren walks through door carrying a large bouquet of pink peonies my favorite and big bottle of SMART water. Before she can speak my doctor walks in behind her.

Dr. Reeves starts to explain that I had an Arthroscopic Meniscectomy which is an outpatient minimally invasive surgical procedure used to treat a torn meniscus cartilage in the knee. The meniscus is often torn as a result of sport-related injury in athletic individuals, like me. Only the torn segment of the meniscus is removed. "You will need assistance from physical therapists postoperatively-4-6 weeks, three times a week.", the doctor explains. "Other than that, you will need to stay here for about an hour in the recovery room and then you can leave." "Jana will set you up with crutches." "I am going to write you another prescription for OxyContin for 60 tablets, take them as directed, no more, no less." "I will see you back in three days to take a look at your knee to be sure that you are healing."

After about an hour of feeling drowsier than I have ever felt before, Lauren takes me home.

She has already been in my house, I can tell, the fresh flowers in my favorite Waterford vase on the kitchen island, peonies of course, a 24 pack of Deer Park water in my pantry, the laundry folded neatly stacked on my little antique bench in my foyer, the curtains and blinds pulled open to welcome me home. "The bed or the couch," she asks? "I would like to stay in the living room and maybe watch a little TV and I am a bit hungry." "Great," Lauren responds, "I am hungry too." After a lot of debate, we decide to order Chinese food. Our favorite order as best friends are always the same, Kung Pao Chicken, fried rice, and Crab Rangoon.

Lauren goes to my fridge and pours herself a glass of Pinot Grigio. "I want one, please." "You just had surgery three hours ago and are on OxyContin, I don't think so." I beg and she acquiesces and pours me a small glass. "That is more like it." I speak. Friends always helping friends, even in wine.

"Let's watch a movie," I suggest. We queued up Netflix and chose a romantic comedy something with Rebel Wilson.

I do not even remember watching the movie because I conk out hard. I am drooling when I awake. I am dreaming about being on a boat on open water and the boat has no anchor. I will go for a swim anyway. I am struggling to get back on the boat, dog paddling and flailing in the chilly, rough waters. The sun blinded my eyes, the water rising to my chin. My fighting the water suddenly abates and I go under the blue azure blanket of waves, vanishing from the surface and the boat's view. Water enters my lungs and fills me, as my body fails to prevent water from entering inside it. I have this feeling that I am drowning as I feel **tearing and burning in my lungs**. Those feelings are followed by feelings of calmness and tranquility. I am floating now back to the water's surface, but no one sees me dead, not even the boat. Bobbing like an apple in a barrel. No one saw me die, no one knows my pain. The irony of life, we do not know each other's pain.

I was awake on the couch when Lauren jumps out of the chair and the credits roll on the movie I did not watch. "My God, are you ok," she asks? "I had a dream, a nightmare, I was drowning all alone." "I actually felt the water enter my lungs, it burned, it was so real." "I told you not to have the wine on the meds you are taking," Lauren scolded. "Come on, let me get you upstairs and to bed." "I have to leave now I have a couple of appointments, but I will call and check on you later," says Lauren.

Lauren had changed the sheets and made my bed like a picture from a magazine. This was always her way. She helped me into bed, left my phone and a glass of water on my nightstand along with medicine. She bought a mini fridge and put it right next to my bed stocked with deli meats. yogurt, cheese, fruit, and water, so I did not have to go downstairs to get anything to eat or drink, she even bought me my favorite Doritos----the blue bag. She kisses me on the cheek and leaves. Lauren is the only real family I have any more except for Eddie. My kids are grown and away and my parents both have died, I have no brothers or sisters so literally Lauren has become my whole world. I feel helpless in this moment, but if I really needed to, I could get down the stairs, but I really did not need to. I had everything that I needed here in my bedroom. TV, phone, Laptop, food, drink, medication. I decided to get up and attempt to take a quick shower or at least rinse off and put on my Pjs. I needed to do that for myself, I felt funky and meddled in surgical filth. I grab my crutches and make my way into my bathroom turn on my shower and undress. Lauren put the trash bags and rubber bands right on my vanity so that my dressings would not get wet. I remember what the nurse showed me. I slide my thin leg into the trash bag and slide the rubber band up over my knee, it holds perfectly.

The shower is just what I needed; I even have enough energy to shampoo my hair. After my shower I just put on a pair of panties and a tee shirt.

I fumble and scoot back into my bed, I feel lonely and think about what next? This is the part of being divorced that really sucks, being all alone when you are in a precarious spot, and really could use the company or even the help. But I have learned that there are pros and cons to everything and in divorce, many, many, more cons than pros.

I pick up my laptop and start to look at social media, but quickly become bored. I then reach for my remote control and flip on my 52-inch TV. I check out the news and then switch to a movie with Tommy Lee Jones. I am ancy, I want a glass of wine, do I dare try and tackle the stairs to go down and get it? Maybe an OxyContin, but I am not due for three more hours, so after much internal debate I decided to try the stairs. I am in some pain and discomfort after all. I make it to the top of the stairs on my crutches with ease, getting down them will be another story.

I made a judgement call. I slide the crutches one by one down the stairs and they land at the bottom with a skirted thud waiting here for me to come and retrieve them.

I take the stairs one by one hopping on my good leg and foot, holding the railing for dear life. I make it down, I hold the wall, lean over, and collect my crutches, I manage to get in my kitchen and wink at my peonies. I fill a water bottle with Pinot Grigio and ascend the staircase. It takes me almost ten minutes to do so and when I hit the top of the staircase, I sit down in my little occasional chair in the hallway for a breath, before heading toward my bedroom. I am sweating, trembling, this took it out of me.

I flop into my bed and swing my bad leg first followed by the other leg. I gulped the Pinot like water and after about five minutes, that Tommy Lee Jones movie was looking like a winner.

After the movie is over and I am almost drunk with pleasure, I take a water bottle out of my mini fridge and take my OxyContin. I hobble one last time to the bathroom then it is lights out and I am all of sudden exhausted, mind, body, and soul. I fall asleep instantly in my clean, cozy bed.

I am deep into my REM sleep having another nightmare, this time there is a young girl in the center of my dream. We are at the Holly Oaks Country Club where I work in Farmington, Connecticut. She is wearing a pink gown and she has a braid in the back. Long, willowy for her age, almost a woman, on the cusp, but not quite. I think she is seated eating cake, in the dining room at the Club.

Virtually every Country Club, with which I'm familiar, requires members to spend significant dollars monthly on its dining facility. It ensures that there will be a steady clientele and consistency of staffing and work hours. It makes job stability far more likely in a Country Club than in any restaurant. So that means that our Country Club dining room is always filled with people we know, for the most part, and this girl I am dreaming about is someone I know, I have seen before at the Club. I am trying too hard to remember her, I can see her face now, clearer, and clearer she becomes to me. I recognize her now through my dreams. She is Tiffany Garrett, daughter of Matt Garrett, our junior Congressmen for Connecticut. She is sweet, innocent and very beautiful; she shines. Matt Garrett had just been elected to Congress and he is only thirty-seven. He beat the senior Congresswoman, Eileen Page who had served great state for nearly twenty years, so last year she retired after her husband died. The Garrett family is happy, laughing, mom, dad, Tiffany! There is a cake and laughing and clapping, a celebration of some kind.

The Garretts were the royal couple of the Farmington Country club, well bred, well educated, rich of course, but not so much nouveau riche; old Connecticut money. When they walked in it was always a head turning event followed by a lot of ass kissing. They were heavy bats and monetary contributors. They were the Farmington

Country club, and everyone knew it. Eddie could not stand Mr. or Mrs. Garrett, he said they were nose bleeds, and always rude to staff, especially the landscapers or anyone in the kitchen. Eddie was right often, but never haughty.

I wake up briefly and see that it is not 2:00a.m. and I roll over on my remote and some infomercial is blaring loudly. I turn it off and roll over and drift back to sleep not before seeing what I thought were black puffy shadows on my bedroom wall. They were saying come dance with me, I will not hurt you. At first, I thought something was on fire and my heart skipped a beat. I smell faint smoke. I did not know it then, but maybe that should have been my first sign of all things evil to come. The Witching Hours take hold of my bedroom, the Devil himself front and center.

The modern significance of the Witching Hour lies in **new beginnings** and the veil between worlds ---- however the original significance may have more to do with secrecy than anything else. The cover of darkness, moonlit or otherwise, allows those who wish to move unseen the cover to do so. The devil is in the details. The Devil's Hour, referring to the time between from **3 a.m. to 4 a.m.** or the hours between midnight and 3 a.m. Some believe this is mumbo jumbo, others choose to believe in the Witching Hour, there are evil spirits and that they cast spells upon the wicked at this time. The spirits of the damned are actually let free during these hours and they walk the earth casting their aspersions and iniquitous wishes upon the living, true evil in its purest form, makings of the Devil itself. Whether I choose to believe it or not, the Witching Hours Lullaby casts a spell over me right then and there.

I fall back asleep lulled by OxyContin and Pinot, I am back in my dream now and Tiffany is the ladies' room, I can hear talking to the girls in there about a boy she likes at the Club, a new bus boy who is smoking hot! "He has a nice package and great butt," she says. She is already wearing a ton of make-up as she applies more lip liner. "I think I want to fuck him or at least blow him," they all laugh together like a joke being told and the punch line being funny. "Have you girls ever played the choking game?" "No, what is that," one of them asks? Tiffany says, "Well, it is a sexual foreplay game when you choke your partner until they almost pass out, it is supposed to release sex hormones and make sex better." "No way," says one of the girls. The other girl in the bathroom, well her mouth drops open. "Let's play one time, who can we get?" Tiffany says, "The guys that work in the kitchen, I bet they are up for some fun. "I know these girls too, although I cannot make them out right now, but they are too familiar. Their silly voices in unison about making some big mistakes.

These girls are in danger! This is only their lives' they are laughing about, and one of them will be dead soon. Beware you dewy-eyed guileless fools, your innocence is what he feeds on and you are his quasi-prime fare. He is on the hunt and you pretty girls are his prey.

I am restless again and want to kick off my sheets so my feet and legs can breathe, but my bad knee will not let my leg move. I am sweating, my lips are salty, I lick them now; I can sense this.

I am back in my dream now and I see Tiffany again. This time she is laying on her back somewhere dark and her dress is torn, her nose bleeding and she is crying hard. I can sense and see she is beneath the moonlight and there are trees around her, many trees. I feel the water again from my first dream and the sense of drowning. She is drowning maybe, I can't make anything out, but I feel the sensation of not being able to breathe.

Her soft voice muffled with pain. Next, I see a garrote around her neck being pulled tighter and tighter, she cannot breathe, she, can't breathe. He is going to kill her and just as I awake up, and I know she is dead.

My first night home was horrible, the pain combined with these weird dreams, but I awaken to a better morning, my knee is still stiff, but I am able to move it more freely and apply a tiny bit of pressure. I wonder about my dreams last night and why I was dreaming about Tiffany Garrett? I reach for my water bottle and take my next OxyContin. I have been feeling strange since taking these pills, I am going to call my doctor this morning. Is it the Oxy, making me hallucinate or the I am actually having visions about Tiffany, the young girl from the Country Club, is this real, even an epiphany?

I manage to get dressed and get downstairs, I make myself a Cup of coffee and turn on the news. Maybe this day will have promise. I start googling the side effects pf OxyContin and one source says that women, especially over fifty, can have hallucinations and bad dreams from the drug. Mumm, that is all it is, I am sure!

I am pouring cream into my black coffee when the story is on the news. Local girl Tiffany Garrett, daughter of our Junior Congressmen Matthew Garrett, was found brutally raped and murdered behind the Holly Oaks Country Club in the woods. There was an eyewitness who saw a young man about six feet tall, slim build wearing a white shirt and dark pants emerging from the woods at that time. Investigators are asking anyone for help if they may know anything?

My coffee mug hits the floor, coffee and creamer splatter the baseboards and faux hard wood. I bend over in two like I am trying to fold myself up and disappear, I almost collapse, but my island saves me, my crutches skirt the floor. My head is hot, and my legs go numb, I am dizzy, I hit the kitchen floor with a thump, narrowly escaping hitting my head on the island. I lay there in a circle, crutches, and all for who knows how long, until Lauren lets herself in and finds me.

Did I just have a premonition of a murder, was what I dreamt about real? Is this perturbation real or an uneasy sickness? The black shadows suddenly appear on my kitchen walls, light and floaty, coming for me, needing to share a secret. I feel an evil presence. The evil is almost comforting, non-malicious, seeking refuge from their own pain. What is going on? Why me, why any of this?

The next thing I know, Lauren is in my kitchen "Wake up, Anna.," "Anna, can you hear me?" I lift up my arm and speak in a voice not my own, "she is dead, Tiffany Garrett, she is dead."

CHAPTER TWO

Dare to Dream

Hold fast to dreams
For if dreams die
Life is a broken-winged bird
That cannot fly
Bruised and broken
Mallow and shy
Soars too low
Fallen from the sky

Little birdie, little birdie, tweet, tweet, little birdie! The chirping outside my bedroom window was from the little family of American Robins who moved in and built their little home, (nest) right next to my window's ledge. Sweet chirping, like the last primal wakeup call beckoning all creatures living.

The hunt is on for Tiffany's killer, but no concrete leads yet. The Police are looking for a bus boy that never showed up for shifts, a man named Victor Guðmundsdóttirr from Iceland. After he missed two shifts, the manager called him, but he never responded. It was as if he just disappeared.

The whole staff, including the landscapers and bellhops are being interviewed, hoping for anything to turn up. The Police put together a sketch that was all over the news and posted everywhere through downtown Farmington, in every bookstore, coffee shop and McDonalds and of course at the Club.

All attention though seems to be on this new kitchen boy Victor, he matched the description given and people who knew him said he was squirrelly and highly compulsive. He had only been a bus boy for a short period of time, a new hire, nobody even knew well. The Club knows that Victor moved here from Maine about a year ago and an acquaintance of one of the dishwashers got him the job here. He came from Bar Harbor Maine where he was running fish with a few distant family members. He hails from Kópavogur, Iceland and from what is known was only in Maine for a brief time before coming to Connecticut. As far as the Police know, he has been in the United States about two, two and half years, but has simply vanished into thin air after Tiffany was killed.

There was not much DNA left on the scene, but a sperm sample taken from Tiffany and a few small drops of blood that did not belong to the victim, which was O+, Tiffany's was O-. The sperm sample came from only one person though. This indicated to the Police that there may have been more than one person involved, or just one man-----many unanswered questions.

The town of Farmington collectively is weeping and broken, everyone is feeling the loss of Tiffany and a killer on the loose. The Club shut down for an entire weekend to mourn the loss of one of their own, and the news says that Matthew Garrett has taken a leave of absence from Congress.

Tiffany's funeral arrangements have been made and publicized. Her name and story are just everywhere. That is the thing about Holly Oaks, we are a big family, when one of our is hurting; we all mourn. Nothing is the same here anymore, like a dark cloud smothering its own.

I am going to the doctor today. It is time for her to change my dressing and look at my knee. Lauren is coming over to pick up in twenty minutes and I am getting ready. The mundane chores of my day are getting easier, dressing myself, fixing meals, showering. I am still on the crutches, but my doctor mentioned a knee brace soon for walking and I can finally ditch the crutches. I am trying to keep my OxyContin on schedule, but I am still in some pain. After the dreams I had about Tiffany I tried to stop taking the OxyContin and just use aspirin, but very quickly found myself back on the Oxy, the pain is still with me from my injury and surgery.

I hear Lauren at the door, "Hey gorgeous you ready, do you need any help?" "No, I will be right down." "Are you sure you are ok, Anna, I am worried about you, you need some TLC." "Hey, let's do lunch at the Honey Bear today after the doctor, my treat," says Lauren. "Sounds perfect," I shout!

The doctor is completely pleased with my knee. She says after the healing process and PT is me to try it out and walk around her office. I am a little weak at first but continue to be well enough to get my doctor's approval. She prescribes more OxyContin and asks me how the pain is? "I am still in some pain, and piercing, burning at times," I say. "Stay on the OxyContin until I see you in two weeks and we will reevaluate your pain then."

Lauren and I order Lobster Cobb salads and peach ice teas at Honey Bear, our favorite restaurant in Farmington, next to the Club of course! Lauren is a member of the Club and has been for five years, she is married, but her husband Al travels three weeks out of the month, in exchange for Al being gone so much, he has made them millionaires, many times over, no kids-----no responsibilities, except to one another. She is certainly in better financial shape than I and often pays for things as she did for lunch today and that was not cheap.

After lunch we went to Elaine's on Barker Street, our favorite retail therapy spot and between the both us, we spent twelve hundred dollars, Lauren's treat again. I got a new pair of boots for the impending Connecticut fall, two pairs pf jeans and a crop top sweater. It felt so good to feel normal again and in the game of life. Lauren was my lifeline and I loved her dearly. Lauren was not a traditionally beautiful woman, a freckled face, crow's feet, prematurely though, and she was tall and thin, too thin even. But with all of these things, Lauren was beautiful to me.

We drove home in Lauren's convertible Mercedes with the top down, letting the wind run through my hair made me feel alive, burning with adrenaline.

Once home I took another OxyContin and told Lauren I needed a nap. She said she was going to stay the afternoon and work from my dining room. Lauren works part time as a party planner for big corporate gatherings. She is good at her job, and it keeps her busy I suppose, but really, she does not have to work, she is financially set for life, thanks to her MIA husband Al. Lauren is a phenom really, everybody likes her, everyone wants to be her.

I begin to drift off to sleep now in my bed now, but I can faintly still hear Lauren on the phone with someone. It brings me comfort, Lauren arguing with someone over something.

I am in back in my dreamscape now, I think I am in a barn, yes, it is almost impossible to mistake anything for a barn. The barn is on fire. There are two horses trapped in the barn, I hear their collective nays. The barn is smoking, and red flames are engulfing the very land it was built upon. It is not just the horses' nays I am hearing now, but a little voice like a scared child. I struggle with my sleep and turn over in the bed taking my bedspread with me. My legs are flailing, even my bad one with the brace.

I see, I see, a young woman lying in the corner covered up with hay. I am back in the water again, the feeling of drowning burning my lungs, unable to breathe. I am interwoven in my dreamscape now, one with it. I am about to come to the climax of this nightmare when I wake up and it is over.

Lauren is standing at the foot of my bed. "Are you ok, I could hear you tossing and turning from downstairs." "Yeah, I think, I just had another nightmare." "Come on let's get you downstairs and we can talk about what to make for dinner, I am just about done with my work." Lauren is a great friend and like family to me. I have two grown kids, who I never see. My son Kevin rarely calls, holidays and birthdays mainly. I did get a text from him asking about how my surgery went. My daughter

Steph is living in Seattle, it might as well be China, I never see her, she is living with a man she met at a bar for about a year ago, and since he moved in, the communication really stopped.

"Oh, by the way," says Lauren, "Eve Rainer called while you were out and she and Sara want to bring you by something later today, I told them you would call back." I did call back, and they said they had made a casserole and homemade chocolate chip cookies and wanted to bring them by. I told them to stop by anytime.

The doorbell rang within the hour, boy that moved fast. Lauren answered the door. "Please come in Eve and Sara, Anna is the kitchen." I was seated at the island on a high bar stool with my leg brace in their full view. "Oh, please let me take that from you," says Lauren. "That is my famous family shared recipe, taco casserole, I hope you like spicy, it like a sort of Mexican lasagna, if you will," says Eve.

Sara grabs a cookie from the porcelain tray her mother sat on my island. "I am looking forward to getting back on the court with you Ms. Davis," she says. "I have been working on my back hand every day since your accident, just like you taught me and because of that, I made the Varsity Team!" "Oh Sara, that is just great and I am so proud of you." This is why I set out to teach tennis in the first place, students like Sara!

"Well," says Eve, "I think we should let Anna rest." "Thank you for stopping by it meant a lot to me." "Oh, by the way," says Eve, "I brought your next payment for the lessons, I know it isn't due quite yet, but thought that maybe under the circumstances you could use it now." "You will let us know when you are ready to return?" "I will, but it could be two more months." "No worries, just get well and whole," she says, "Bye for now Anna." "Bye Eve, bye Sara, and thank you for the food."

The company and day wore me out. After dinner Lauren helps me change into my favorite pajamas and heads home. It is nine pm and I had a big day and I am exhausted.

No TV or social media for me tonight. I take my next dose of OxyContin and turn my lamp off and pray for an easy, peaceful night of sleep.

I nod off into a lavender haze or is it a hillside with lavender flowers, what could they be, maybe it was Wisteria. The sky aligned with a light purple hue and dominated the views. I like being in this dreamscape, I could almost smell the scent of the Wisteria when….. I am back at the burning barn. The barn is almost burned down to the ground. I am looking for those horses and that small woman, but see nothing anymore, the smoke almost hurts my eyes as I wake up with a thundering scream. I look at my clock and it says its 3am again, the shadows are back on the wall and this time they seem more present in a deliberate way. Making their way through my bedroom and swirling like a cloud on top of me, I feel heat and anger, I am petrified.

I sit up in my bed numb, not moving a muscle, maybe not even breathing until I hear the shadows speak directly to me. Their arrogant, direct voices bounced off me like a raindrop off an umbrella, and then through me like a dagger. Jenna Parker was the name they said!

Jenna Parker was homecoming queen at Farmington High School last year and was a freshman at the University in Storrs, Connecticut, she was just home for the summer with her family. I had run into her and her family many times at the Club this past summer. This girl was going places, not only beautiful, smart and a good family girl, but also, Ms. Connecticut Teen, pageantry was in her blood. The Farmington Country Club ONLY produced these kinds of people.

I think I pass out, my dreams thicken, and I see her face now and she is wearing her crown and waving to her crowd, this is the parade in Farmington for Jenna after she won Ms. Teen Connecticut last year. This was a Farmington tradition complete with a convertible car, roses, a sash, and crown; she sparkled, she was so special. My eyes move away from her, I can see a dark cloud, more like a presence in the crowd at the parade. I could see a man, he was tall, slender, hunched over, but good looking in the face. His bone structure was what made him so handsome, unique;

almost European. I know him, I have seen that face before. Back now to Jenna in the red convertible, her pink satin gown flowing in the light breeze. Her blonde curls bouncing off her back and shoulders. She is so innocent, like a budding flower, soaking up her moment like the flower soaking up the sun.

Someone is stalking her; someone wants her in a different way. Someone is looking to capture her, kill her and kill her essence, someone hates her. He hates all women like her, just for being special, when they are not. Someone so sinister they wish to punish and eliminate anyone who has what they do not; the spotlight, opportunity, money, and advantage; dripping with privilege.

When all of a sudden, the car stops moving, the people stop clapping, and the thunder and rain starts. The heavy downpour washes away Jenna's moment and the image of his face. People scuddle and run for cover, the rain washes away all sense of her, of him.

I am now back at the burning barn. I see the flames have now engulfed everything and banished it whole, only smolder and smoke are left. In the fragments of my dream, I see bones, and burned clothes and hair, I can see the long blonde curled hair matted in cinder and pain, long, bouncy curls just like the curls bouncing in the convertible in that Parade.

She is gone! I wake up screaming she is gone, she burned to death in that barn, Oh My God! I shake my head, like a dog shedding water after its bath, shaking my mind like a martini, but the visions stay with me, my head teetering on my shoulders; my dream is real.

She had been missing for three days now, the community, Police and anyone who lived in Farmington and the surrounding areas all looking for her. Jenna Parker just gone missing. Just like Tiffany Garrett. We have a serial killer stalking out little town and for some reason I am smack dab in the middle of it all.

It has been 24 hours since my dream about Jenna and the face in the crowd. That face I recognize it, a big nose, high cheekbones, raised forehead; European. The day had faded on and I did not leave or speak to anyone, I was simply too afraid to. The sky had turned grey and befallen into dusk and putting a cover on all her secrets. I am about to go to bed, scared to death of what my next dream may reveal. I am sipping my second glass of wine and pop an OxyContin to relieve me of any anxiety. I still have a third of the bottle left and I am dreading when the bottle goes empty. My doctor will likely not prescribe me anymore Oxy as I am healing and really don't even need them. The combo of my wine and Oxy is euphoric and warm, changing, changing my thinking, my brain. I will hate to have this feeling leave me soon and know I cannot ever get it back. I am buzzed now, like a hug from the top of my head to the bottom of my feet. I feel slushy, all gooey and mellow. In my moments of haze and a narcotized state, my mind presents to me a blank canvas. All my memories washed away and nonrational thought left behind me, as I slump in the chair I am seated in three feet from bed. I feel like I may just pass out here, I am so droopy and tired, but my body tightens, and I sit up as I see and hear simultaneously put the name Victor right in front of me.

I am thinking and thinking about what to do. I have not told anyone about my dreams, not even Lauren. I decide I cannot keep this information to myself, even if may sound crazy, I decide I have to call the Police.

I pick up the phone and call the non-emergency Police number in Farmington and a woman named Lois answers.

All of a sudden, I can't speak, my throat is dry and my lips pucker, as I struggle to find the words to say to Lois. My little voice comes through though and does not betray me, as I speak the vile, barbarous words into the phone. "I am Anna Davis and I think I know who may have hurt Tiffany Garrett and Jenna Parker."

The next thing I know is that the Police are knocking on my door loudly the dead could hear, shining bright lights through every window in my townhouse until I came to.

"I am coming." I yell. I stumbled for my robe and then down the stairs, finally to the door with the loud banging and circus lights.

I answer the door. "Are you Anna Davis?" The male police officer asks me in a demanding tone. "Yes." "We got a dispatch from out call center that you placed a call to the non-emergency police department and left a message with a Lois Walker, that you perhaps have information about the death of Tiffany Garrett and another girl, Jenna Parker who is missing? "I am Office Jack Pell and this Officer Simone Banks, may we come in?"

"I think I do," I say as drool forms up in the corner of mouth, and I think am I awake? "Please come in."

I offer seats to the officers and a beverage; both were met with a "no thank you." "I am Anna Davis, and I am home recuperating from outpatient surgery on my knee, I have been home about a week now." The officers look around my living room and then scan what they can see in the kitchen, they see two open wine bottles on the kitchen island. "Do you drink, Ms. Davis," asks the female officer. "I do from time to time, but I am on OxyContin right now for my post-surgical pain, so I am not supposed to really be drinking alcohol." "OxyContin" asks the male officer?"

"Yes, I have been taking it regularly it does help with the pain, and I only have ten pills left." "What does that have to do with these missing girls" I ask? "Look---- when I go to bed at night between 1am-4am I have the same dream, the first dream was about Tiffany Garrett and now the second dream about Jenna Parker." "She is still missing?"

"I have a bad feeling about Jenna," I say. "The witching hours, both dreams are during the witching hours, interesting?" The female officer nods her head and cracks her neck. "What else," she asks? "Anything about the dream about Jenna?"

"Well, I start out." "The first dream was about Tiffany Garrett, I saw her lying on the cold, dark ground in the woods behind the Holly Oaks Country Club, I saw a young man there too." "He had a European look about him, slim face, high cheek bones." "I remember a name came to me, Victor, has there been any mention or information about someone named Victor since Tiffany's death?" "The second dream was more abstract, I saw a blonde woman in my dreams, she had been burnet, she was in an old barn somewhere, and that barn had been burnt to the ground, smoke and embers everywhere, but I could see through their clouds of pain." "I also dreamt about her Parade in town for winning Miss Teen Connecticut, the same man was there, at least I think so." "He had the same face, European looking and that was over a year ago."

"Ok, so you are having dreams, this is hardly evidence Ms., Davis." "I can't take this to the station and pursue it without any evidence." "Could you at least look into someone associated with or around the Country Club named Victor?" "Can you at least look for an old barn that has been burnt down, before it is too late for Jenna," I ask?

"Ms. Davis, calm down please and let us determine what, of anything, needs to be done." "There are no barns in within a thirty-mile radius of Farmington, anyhow," says the male officer? "We have nothing to go on." "Do you watch horror movies," asks the female officer? "Why?" "You are not possibly thinking that I had something to do with these missing girls, or that it is all in my head, do you?"

"I have your information and we may be back in touch and if anything, else comes up give us a call." The Police got up fast and are leaving even faster. "Thank you," I say and show them the door. As they step through my threshold, they get a call on their walkie. Something about a barn that was burnt down, and a body found, a young teenage female. They both leave in a rush leaving me standing there in suspense, waiting, waiting for God knows what? My body folds in half and I cannot catch air, I nearly collapse. They rush off hurriedly, with the shades of blue fading in their fury.

I am back in the azure blue water now, near the boat with no anchor, I am drowning, I am dying, help me, please.......

I stumble back inside, lock the door, and crawl the stairs up to my bedroom, I lock that door too and jump into my bed. I pull my covers tight as if to hug me and lull me to sleep and stop all the horrific spinning. I take my next OxyContin and settle deep into my mattress, there it is, I will be asleep soon.

I am humming to myself now just waiting for the witching hours to come and sing me my lullaby.

I wake up around 2:15am and I am panicked, I did not have any dreams that I can remember, but I am scared. I sense a presence in my bedroom, the feeling that I am not alone. I take a sip of water and actually yell out into my room, but there is dead silence. I open my eyes wider, and I think I can see someone sitting in the chair across the room from me. The same one I was sitting in just a few hours ago. A big presence even more than any man could ever be. I sit quietly and finally it rises and is upon me, it sits near me on my bed. I am so anxious and scared I pee my panties and soil the mattress beneath me. My knee starts to ache, my mouth is fuzzy and my tongue heavy especially when I ask, "What do you want from me?"

The monster turns to me, and its face is directly in front of mine. Its eyes fire red, its face no shape or form, but I knew it was Satan. "He spoke directly to me and said, Tiffany Garrett, Jenna Parker, Elise Frank." "I killed those girls." The laughing and cackling continued from the monster until it vanished into thin in air and all that was left behind was a foul smell, like rotten eggs and the knowing of what happened here was real. There was no trace of him or it, except for a small droplet of blood left behind on the cushion of my chair.

The next morning Lauren comes over and we are going to see my doctor for a check up on my knee and ask to come off the OxyContin. The dreams are getting too wild, too big for me to handle.

Lauren is right on time and greets with the biggest Lauren bear hug! She had a gift bag and a card for me. "Go ahead and open it now, silly," she says. Inside was a Louis Vuitton small clutch and an elegant get-well card. "From many of us at the

Club, you are loved by many." "Now let's grab some coffee and a scone before we see your doctor."

We stopped at Elaine's, a local favorite for honey scones and cappuccinos. Lauren orders half a dozen scones to go. Once in the car Lauren starts in on me. "So, what are these dreams you have been having and how are the Police involved? "Everyone at the Club knows and people are talking." "Are you in any trouble Anna, what do you know about these girls?" "Let me get a word in Lauren.," I say.

"I have been having dreams, more than that really, visions and last night an image of Satan came right up to me in my bed." "Oh My God, and said what?" "It just cackled and laughed and told me he killed three girls and gave me all three of their names." "What did the Police say?" "They don't know about the new dream last night; I want to talk to the doctor first and get some guidance about all of this." "I want to come off of the Oxy too." "Do you think the OxyContin might have something to do with these visions?" "I don't know Lauren, I honestly do not know anything anymore, except what is happening is real and from what I can sense, not over."

We are both seated in the doctor's examine room right away, but Lauren receives a phone call excuses herself. My doctor comes in ten minutes later. "Well, let's take a look at that knee?"

"All is healing well and how are you on your pain meds?" "Doctor, if it is all right, I would like to stop taking the OxyContin, I have been having bizarre dreams and thoughts." "We can stop the OxyContin today, but if you are still in any pain, you must continue on Tylenol." "I am about to start you on physical therapy and if you are in any pain, your exercises may be too tedious for you and you must do the therapy." "I understand doctor thank you."

She then handed me a list of physical therapists to schedule my therapy and highlighted the ones she recommends.

"Doctor, on a different note, what do you know about OxyContin and dreams or hallucinations?" "Well, I know that OxyContin can disturb dreams and sleep." "Hallucinations occur only in the full waking state. Yet similarities to sleep-related experiences such as hypnagogic and hypnopompic hallucinations, dreams, and parasomnias, have been noted since antiquity." "Almost any medication, especially Opioids when mixed with alcohol can cause extreme side effects and hallucinations." "So, let us try the Tylenol going forward and see if that doesn't help and limit any alcohol consumption to a half a glass a day." "Will do Doc" and thanks. As I was leaving the Doctor's office Lauren suddenly shows up and grabs my hand and we walk out in a rush. She pulls me down the hall and drags me in the elevator, when we finally get to the parking lot, she tells me to just get in the car.

Once in the car I really let her have it, "You could have hurt me, I am still unstable on my feet, what the hell Lauren?"

She puts her hand on my shoulders and looks me in my eyes, I can still smell the scones and cappuccino on her breath. "They found Jenna Parker in that old Barn on Highway Four." "The barn had been burned down with her in it, she is dead, it is all over the news."

"I knew it, I knew it," I shouted for all to hear. "I knew it!" With all my shouting and ranting, my breathing begins to abate, and I am running out of air. Who am I anymore?

I am back in the water now, the water is about to cover my mouth and nose right before I go under, the azure blue of the water is all I see. It does not pain me; the rich warm water lulls me in comfort singing its lullaby for only me to hear.

I am back in the present now, but still cannot breathe. Choking in my newfound knowledge. The air is buzzing and whirling around my head, and I see pink spots, then black ones, and just like that I pass out, sitting straight up in my best friend's car.

CHAPTER THREE

The Killings

Upon the threshold, red-eyed Murder stands,
Fresh from his slaughter-house of human meat,
Blood on his broken teeth and on his hands,

Blood on his nails and on his purple feet.
With hollow voice he speaks, and sickening breath,
A way there is, that only way is death!
The dead will rise no more, -the dead are dead!
The spared will creep behind your back instead.

I am taken to the emergency room by Lauren where my doctor meets us in about thirty minutes. I am delusional and having a hard time catching a deep breath. My breathing is consistent, but shallow and I fear I am not able to catch enough breath to sustain myself. The azure water is with me here. I close my eyes and can actually smell the salt in her.

The ER doctor, (Mica is his name and he looks about 12) tells my doctor about my status and turns over my file to her. Dr. Radcliff steps in the place now of an untutored, green doctor who has moved on down the hall.

Dr. Radcliff says that my attack is due to the OxyContin being in my system and has removed all opioids from my diet, but the effects can still linger. I am free to go home once the doctor clears me and fills out some paperwork.

Lauren takes me home with a look of OMG, what just happened here?

"You could have died Anna; let's get you well and starting PT and back to work." "You need your normal life back now, all of the nightmares and strange occurrences, well, it is all too much."

Once home and in my own bed with a bottle of smart water, and Lauren lying next to me watching TV made me relax. "Lauren," I ask? "Yes," she replies. "Is there something wrong with me?" "I think it was just what Dr. Radcliff said to you, you have been having a bad reaction to your medication and that combined with the rigors of your surgery and your body trying to heal, has just been too much." "Maybe," I say. Lauren grabs my hand and just like that two best friends fall asleep side by side.

We awoke to the TV blasting and my front door being nearly beaten in. I look out of my bedroom window and see three police officers and flashing blue lights still flashing in their Pontiacs.

Lauren runs downstairs and lets them in. The first police officer storms in the same one who had been here before about my dreams when I called them, Officer Pell, the other two officers followed in, but I didn't recognize either of the, both women. "We are here to ask you questions about the murder of Jenna Parker." "Did you know Ms. Parker, her family?" "You worked at the Country Club where her family has been members for four years, did you know them?" "Wait a second here," says Lauren, "is my friend a suspect?"

"We have found the body of Jenna Parker in the old barn on Highway Four." "Someone set that barn on fire and killed Ms. Parker." "We are waiting on the cause of death from the coroner now but be assured Ms. Parker died in that barn and you somehow--- you knew about it."

"I don't think I should answer any more questions without a lawyer." "Well then Ms. Davis, you better get one." "We will need you to buy at the station at 9am tomorrow morning." The officers file into a single line and just a marching band, march right out of my front door.

"See you and your lawyer tomorrow at 9am sharp, good night Ms. Davis."

"Ok, who do we know that is a lawyer from the Club?" "I know," says Lauren, "Ed Garcia, he hit on me a couple of times, you know the fat, balding guy, with the pregnancy gut and the topee." "Yes, he is supposed to be a real shark and probably dying to help a couple of damsels in distress." "I will call him," says Lauren.

Ed has agreed to meet us at 9am the next morning at the station to represent me. Lauren says she will cover whatever bill Ed comes up with.

Lauren says she is going to stay the night with me so that we are both fresh and ready to go into the station the next morning. She says she is going to the grocery store to pick up some things and she will be back in about an hour.

I walk upstairs, still in knee brace, to take a nap.

I fall onto my bed, every muscle of being screaming until I pass out back in my dreamscape, where I am anything but safe.

This time my dream takes me to a bar, a local bar, I know it, Macabees, a real local joint. Everyone goes there, the kind of bar/restaurant place with great burgers and beer.

I see an underage young woman flirting with a man, but their backs are to me, and I cannot make out their faces. Their body language is saying they like each other and are sexually into one another. Macabees is near the pavilion in downtown Farmington. The pavilion is located in the heart of Downtown Farmington adjacent to Riley Park. The Park was named after George F. Riley who, through The Riley Foundation, donated the funds for its construction. Perhaps the best-known park event is Rhythmz in Riley Park. This summertime concert series is attended by about five hundred each Friday, June-August. We are there now in my dream. The same young woman and man are there listening to the music and holding hands.

They are drinking from a flask, and her heads snaps back with laughter, he must have said something funny. I can almost hear the music in my dream, loud and obnoxious, yet soothing and surreal. The night was almost too perfect, representative of a looming cataclysm rooted in a vicissitude, heading right towards this naive young woman. This man was too familiar to me, something about his presence, his face even though I cannot see him. Maybe this is the same man in all of my dreams? I try so hard to pay attention to all of the details my dreams are serving to me, any little detail missed, I may not be able to piece this information together.

The night went dark, my dream moves faster and faster and then, I see it; his face, bold and sharp with no remorse, almost handsome if you took away his intent, but his intent was there. European, tall, slim, high cheekbones, big nose, yes, it is him!

They are alone now in a dark alley now far away from the pavilion, they are kissing. When I see, I see, him push her to the ground and he starts beating her in the face with his closed fist.

He looks up to the sky with her splattered blood all over his perfect face and I see him so clearly. He is howling at the moon at this moment. A man turned into a wolf like beat, maybe even a werewolf. I do not know him, but I know what is about to happen next, I can sense the sexual awakening though my dream. I become aroused and start rubbing my clitoris and then I am back in the dream, and he is on top of her now pumping hard, and she is screaming. He fucks her raw, she is a little squirmy worm under his manly thrusts. He looked up at the moon with another howl as he came----the werewolf in him fulfilled. His face turns red and void of anything human as he reaches into his pocket and pulls out a hunting knife with a jagged edge. With a quick swish of the knife, her life is gone, she lay there bleeding on the street; alone and cold. Her slit throat bore my own pain, as the killer roars like a lion and I now know Elise Frank is dead.

I am back in the blue azure water about to go under and drown, when I am tossing and turning now and coming out of my dream, with a jolting wake up call, I sit straight up in my bed and scream her name, she is gone forever, his next victim, Elise Frank.

Elise Frank was not as privileged as Tiffany Garrett, or a beauty queen like Jenna Parker, she was average, dowdy even, but from the richest family in Farmington and everyone at the Club worshipped them. They were very well known. Every man wanted them, and every woman wanted to be them.

These three girls that have been murdered, all so different but they share something some things in common; their age, late teens, early twenties, their County Club status and that they were all naïve enough to believe their lives would last forever.

"Lauren, I need help," but she is still at the store, running errands. I reach for my phone and call the officer, Officer Pell, (this time he left me a card with all of his information), he answers right away. I called Ed, my lawyer and Lauren and tell them all to meet me at the station, I have more information.

I dress, pee, and grab my car keys, the first time I have driven in nearly two weeks. I drive with caution to the police station, trying out my new meniscus. Lauren beats me there and is waiting out front. She hugs me immediately and whispers in my ear, "the press is here, they have found another body of a young girl, throat slit near the pavilion-downtown." She wraps her arm around me, and we begin walking in the station, but not before the press is all up on us. "What do you know about the disappearance of Elise Frank?" "What about Tiffany Garrett and Jenna Parker?" Ed Garcia shows up in the nick of time, "no comment," he says.

Ed pulls me and Lauren inside where we are escorted into a room with no windows and pueke colored walls. "Coffee, water or anything?" the woman asks. Ed shakes her off. Office Pell walks into the room. "This is my Captain and superior Dan Betts; he is going to be sitting in on the questioning." Ed agrees with this, and we move on. Office Pell pulls out a tape recorder and sets it on the table and then clears his throat loud enough to wake the dead, then speaks. "Elise Frank has been reported missing, last seen, last night, by her friends at a bar downtown called Macabees." "Any information you may have about the whereabouts of Ms. Frank is crucial at this point."

"I have no information other than I have been having wicked dreams, nightmares really about the killings, images, no more like, visions." "What exactly is my client being retained for, she knows nothing," asks Ed. "Did you know any of these girls?" "What do you mean," I ask? "From the Country Club or from around Farmington," asks Officer Pell. "I knew all of them, their families really from the Country Club, everyone knows Matt Garrett, he our State's Junior Congressmen." "Yes, he is," confirms Office Pell. Ed leans in, "What the hell is this?" "Where are these questions leading?" "We have some camera footage, it is shotty at best and blurred, but hoping maybe Ms. Davis here can help us out." "Camera footage?" "Yes, from behind the Country Club, it shows Tiffany Garrett leaving the club with a young man, tall with dark hair and high cheekbones and a big nose." "Listen, we just want her to look at the footage, see if she recognizes anything, we may have a serial right here in Farmington and out in the community, this is not safe," says Dan Betts. "We can do it," says Ed, he pats my hand. "Let me get the footage set up."

Lauren grabs me by the arm and holds my hand as walk down a small, narrow corridor to a dark room, when all of a sudden, a camera starts rolling likening a home video. It is blurry, spotty, and hard to see, but I can make out Tiffany Garret leaving the club, her dress is impeccable something she would wear to the Club. I see the boy/man right behind her, he looks so young. The seem to know one another by their body language as they walk out the back of the Club side by side and then they were just gone, Tiffany gone forever, and this man becomes who we all seek.

I have seen before, I know him I think, "let me see it again please."

Yes, that face it was the new bus boy, the one all of the girls at the Club had a crush on the one with the handsome European face, what was his name, his name was Victor!

Victor, he is the one.......

Ed and Lauren led me out of the Police Station. The Police have their suspect now and a name to put with that handsome face. Victor, the mysterious bus boy of Farmington, Connecticut, where are you, Victor? Ed and I agreed to be available to help the Police in any way and I promised to call immediately with anymore ne information, but Office Pell and his superior felt confident in their new lead. They had suspected him too and had been investigating the whole Eurotrash click.

I am home now thinking about the day and the torment of it all. Lauren offered to stay with me overnight, but I felt safer alone, these dreams of mine must be interpreted and explained and only I can do that, sometimes it is better to be alone. I love her for wanting to stay, but I just had an intuition I may learn more on this night.

It is again the Witching Hours of the night 3am---- and I am still awake. Tonight, there is no dream, only reality and the realities are looking at me through a red haze of filthy souls. Then the room goes quiet, lifts her veil, and lets the evil in.

The devil himself is sitting in my chair across from my bed, in my own bedroom, why me, I think, why me? He is back and literally on fire in front of my eyes. His shape is moving and on fire at the same time, unrested with bright orange flames.

You people of this earth think you are so righteous, so good, when really you are born of me. All you dirty bitches, who partake in materialism and dirty sex, you idolize things and desire money before anything else, you sluts belong to me." "Your souls will burn in hell because you have no faith in what you can't see or feel." "You have become hopeless, useless, discarded, just the way I like it, so much easier for me to prey upon and devour you."

I am a rebel in revolt against Almighty God. You say, "That's foolish!" Yes, that is foolish. But I have been deceived and twisted by the sinful pride in his heart. The Bible says his wisdom is corrupted because of his pride, and now I am in revolt against Almighty God. My purpose is to literally overthrow God and take all of you sinners and non-believers with me. "Even this who believe in Jesus Christ will submit to me when they lose their faith, and their eyes go black."

"It isn't Victor, you stupid woman, it is me!" "I killed those girls, but I am going to blame him, use you, I am going to torment you until you give what I really want; your eternal soul!"

"You belong to me!"

And just like that, the devil was gone, and he caught my bedroom curtains on fire, departing.

CHAPTER FOUR

The Killer

The murders sweet, attractive smell
Flames the fuel of the pits of hell
I did it right, I did it wrong
Just my urgency to belong
I kill you clean
Dirty no spell
To cast you away
To the pits of hell

Someone she knows

Everyone wants great sex; and everyone is looking for ways to get it. As times come, some things go, somethings stay, but the choking game was never more dangerous than its cousin, begin foreplay. Sex acts like choking — widespread both in porn and real sex — can go totally undiscussed up until it is happening to you, whether your partner's asking you to do it to them, or vice versa. For all the relative unsexiness of the word, which can recall having a piece of food stuck in your throat rather than something you would do in bed, choking is actually something that's a big turn-on for a lot of people, whether that's giving, receiving or both. On the flipside, however, it is also something that's quite dangerous, and if done improperly, could lead to injury, brain damage and even death — meaning, it's a highly dangerous sex act.

To others though, it is the pathway to pure forbidden ecstasy.

Tiffany Garrett was the first victim, she was only eighteen, and just started thinking about becoming a woman and that journey when she was abducted from the Holly Oaks Country Club, raped, and choked. He just had to have her, kill her, take complete control over. That bitch, white girl, so privileged, she had to go, and with brutality he took her life. He wanted to be her, become her, he hated her, all of them who had what he didn't,' privilege, money and love, the good life!

He wanted to carry out these acts upon her but was stopped by someone else who got there first. Someone who in a moment of passion accidentally took Tiffany's life.

Even though Tiffany was a mere eighteen years of age, she looked twenty-five. She has a mature, a knowing, an intelligence about her you could just tell she was going places.

Her father was Matthew Garrett, the first congressmen for the state of Connecticut about to be thirty-nine, the first under forty. Young and eminent, a promising future for that family.

He had been stalking her for almost a year. The same time frame that he had been working at the Country Club as a bus boy. He was titillated and impassioned by the girls at the country Club of a certain age. Sixteen, seventeen; eighteen was pushing too old for him. He preferred the girls that were under sixteen but had to control himself. These girls had access to everything, culture, money, the right people, education, and privilege. He idolized these girls in their fancy party dresses at the club, all dressed up in their real pearl necklaces and earrings, some of them even wore diamonds. He wanted to kiss them, fuck them, murder them, be them! He could not live fully unless they were dead, and he could not function until he licked their blood. He never knew this kind of woman or life before. His mere upbringing did not afford him that and his lack of experience and opportunity drove him to pursue the forbidden.

Victor grew up Victor Guðmundsdóttirr outside of Reykjavik, Iceland, his childhood in Iceland was wonderful and close, summers hiking and fishing and the winter filled with family, neighbors, friends, and the church. For a little island, some call it the little rock of the artic, it was Victor's life.

Iceland is geographically positioned both in the Northern and Western hemispheres of the Earth. Situated just south of the Arctic Circle, Iceland is bordered by the Atlantic Ocean in the south, the Greenland Sea in the north, the Denmark Strait in the northwest and the Norwegian Sea in the east.

Iceland is an island in the Atlantic Ocean, located near the Arctic Circle, between Greenland and Norway. An island of 103.000 km2 (40,000 square miles), it is about the same size as Hungary and Portugal, or Kentucky and Virginia. Iceland is the second largest island in Europe, following Great Britain, and the 18th largest island in the world. The coastline is 4,970 km.

Located just outside of Reykjavik, Kópavogur is the second biggest community in Iceland with just over 30,000 inhabitants and is currently undergoing rapid development. The beautiful Kópavogur Art Museum, which opened just 30 years ago, is a must-visit. Also located just outside of Reykjavik, Hafnarfjörður is the third largest town in Iceland. The Reykjavik town limits about 30-mile in any direction housed its 80% of Iceland's population. Everyone on Iceland was brought together by her fire and ice here and transmuted into family.

Victor Guðmundsdóttirr was from a great family with five brothers and two sisters, eight total, they were not poor but always had to sacrifice and lived on hand me downs, and with him being the youngest, it was anything but glamorous. Salmon fishing on the coast from June to September, dinner on Sundays, church twice a week, choir in the Winter; a good life. Simple, void of all of the trimmings and trappings of the Country Club lifestyle.

It was during one very cold and dark day in October, when there was only four hours of sunlight in a single day, that it happened.

Victor was ice fishing with his uncle off a little pond near his home and the sun was beginning to abate. "Time to pack it up." says his uncle, "sun is gone." But when Victor stood up the slushy ice beneath his feet caved in. He fell through the ice in a nano second unable to breathe, once he hit the water which was 31 degrees his blood froze, and all went black. He could not move his limbs, which only allowed for the water to pull him down faster. The blue azure water was peaceful, mesmerizing, and calm. After a full minute of her presence, he stopped breathing and simply let go.

He did not remember anything after that until he regained consciousness after his uncle pulled him from the ice and gave him CPR. Victor dreamed of a better life and with this experience, he felt he was given a second chance. He will move forward now, taking with him the blue azure water of Iceland as his souvenir. His blood now ran blue and artic with his knowing of a chance for something better, anything more. He learned this while nearly frozen under a sheet of ice.

It was when Victor turned nineteen, he was offered a position working the docks in Bar Harbor Maine, running fish, and helping the deliveries of the fresh catch to be sorted. Victor being an avid fisherman and knew the fishing ropes, he decided to move to Maine with his cousin Aron. It was a chance to get his foot in America's door and learn something new. Victor dreamt of America and would never refuse a chance to take a bite out of her; taste her. His time was now, and what an opportunity.

Bar Harbor Maine was a dream come true for Victor, for anyone. Bar Harbor was happening place in all respects. Tourism, restaurants and chartered fishing, great weather, and great people, cultured and educated, pure New England.

He worked hard in Maine for two summers with his uncle, saved some money--- learned a lot. Then finally they got a real break when his uncle and a friend got offered jobs working in Connecticut on the Piers near Point Beach, lots of people, plenty of tourists, laden with opportunity. That move was exciting, but dangerous at the same time as Victor's uncle's friend was a common thief, pickpocketing tourists, stealing wallets from unassuming people, and even conning a widow out of five thousand dollars. He ended up stealing from the job once there and got caught, and all three of them were canned and suddenly became three men that were penniless and homeless.

Victor's uncle had heard of a Country Club up in Farmington about an hour away that was looking for bus boys, cooks, and car valets. After sleeping in a tent and eating from trashcans for about two weeks, Victor decided something had to give. Victor decided to go up to Farmington and apply for the job, any job, while his uncle and uncle's friend just disappeared, evaporated into thin air, leaving Victor to find his way. Victor never looked back and seized this opportunity. Carpe Diem, he thought, the American Way! His Uncle's betrayal was even understood by him, having to break apart to survive the Grapes of Wrath Way.

Victor slept in abandoned barns and even under bridges along the way. It was the blue azure water of that Iceland fishing hole that held him now, the knowing of a better life and the lessons he learned there. Even the worst things that happen to us can create comfort through their terror. Lessons to be learned, life to manage, a future to find.

Until the day he rolled into Holly Oaks, Victor had never seen anything like the Holly Oaks Country Club. The Club itself was built on five acres, which had a complete 18-hole golf course, two pools, tennis courts, a restaurant, game room and access to the prettiest, youngest debutants and socialites: jackpot. Even though Victor was deemed classless, uneducated, and poor----no one would have to know that here. You could be anybody and make up a life at Holly Oaks, if you were young enough and good-looking enough, who really cared. People were shallow, they didn't need to know your truth as long as you presented well and played the game.

Victor was hired immediately and although he was the only restaurant staff member from Iceland there many from Europe. Cedric another bus boy was from Lativa, Darrs, a waiter was from the Ukraine and Tom, the hostess and seater was from Finland and lastly Paul from Hungry was the dishwasher. Victor got along well with the guys at the Club, work was fun and he was bunking with Tom at his sister's house in Farmington, only two miles away. They all became fast friends. They formed sort of a boy's club at the Country Club nicknamed "Eurotrash." Employees, staff, and members alike knew about them. Bad boys, hot boys, the dangerous kind.

The gang became really popular with the ladies at the Club, young and old alike. Cedric was dating a widow who he hustled 10K from with more to come, they were a bad boys club, scamming women and looking for money. But they had the goods, good looking, young, European and most could fuck you until you could not walk.

The Easter European men especially arriving in the states without a penny to their name were hunger to succeed, feeling like America needs to ration out her pie and these women were the key to their lock, the knife to their slice. All of them were on the hunt looking for it, waiting to seize or steal it or fuck their way into it. The young girls at the Club were the low hanging fruit and presented themselves right for the picking, paradise for them, every father's worst nightmare for their daughters.

Paul, Tom, and Victor went on a double date one time with three of the young girls from the club, one of them was Tiffany Garrett who had been on Instagram with Victor in his Dms. Victor and Tiffany liked one another and made no secret of showing their affection. They all met in the kitchen at the Club and ate and drank the stolen food and wine that Paul and Tom had taken. Paul was with Jenna Parker and Tom was with a girl named Elise Frank, both Country Club girls like Tiffany.

Paul and Tom disappeared into the woods with their dates for what seemed like a long time while Victor and Tiffany got to know one another through the fine art of French kissing. When all of a sudden, Paul and his date emerged from the woods she was screaming and crying and her throat was bright red, as if she had been burned. "Come on Jenna," says Tiffany "Don't be like that he was just trying to show you a good time." "How, by choking me half to death?" Just then Tom emerges from the woods, carrying his Elise in his arms, she passed out cold. "Give me some room," he says and then lays her out flat on the blanket on the ground. "Should we call someone," asks Victor? But no one did anything we all just watched her until she woke and was able to breathe again and when she did, she smiled and said, "Let's do it again." Tom had choked Elise, almost to death and in sexual frustration stopped when he thought he may have hurt her.

Tiffany even told her friends that she was going to play the choking game with Victor and then "fuck his brains out." The "Choking Game" was their revelation, their masterminded sex game and all were victims, and all got fucked. Tiffany was a lead instigator, while Victor and the others were more passive, but willing to participate. They formed a cult that night at the club ready and willing, hungry, and dumb.

Victor grew weary of this and realized that he really liked Tiffany. He could even see potentially them becoming an item. Victor wanted a girlfriend and he was totally into Tiffany. When Victor finally asked her out on a solo date, the date started slowly, as they met at the Club for dinner and then heated up after they left the Club and went into the woods behind the Club's property.

They started drinking from a flask that Victor had brought filled with Icelandic Vodka. Their body language on the patio reeked of sex and seared its wanting. People noticed; people took notes. The two of them stood out, exuding sex and unyielding desire, their hormones could be smelled from fifty feet away, adjacent to their spirits which were tethered in longing. They stepped off the patio into the woods for only a moment, a moment of eternal bliss with no turning back from it.

They found a private area beneath an old Pinchot Sycamore tree beneath the moonlight. The drunker they got; they started fooling around. Their kisses burned the night air and penetrated the moon. They were rounding third base when Tiffany suggested they try something else. She pulled out a garrote from her purse and asked Victor to tie it around her neck and fuck her and to not stop unless she passed out.

Victor felt uncomfortable but was turned on at the same time. "All the kids are doing it," says Tiffany. "I don't know what if I hurt you?" "Let me try it on you first." "Ok," says Victor. Tiffany's garrote was made from a thick rope with handles almost like straps. She slid it around Victor's throat and pulled from behind, Victor immediately started coughing and choking as Tiffany pulled harder and harder until, at last, Victor stopped breathing and she let go. When she did, he gasped for air clutching at his chest. "My God, Tiffany you could have killed me." "Oh, don't be that way handsome." "It was all in fun." All the cool kids are doing it, why are you such a pussy" asks Tiffany?

"Lay me down and fuck me, Victor." To Victor's amazement he was fully erect and ready, Victor unbuckles his pants amazed that he is still erect through the pain of the garrote. His throat is raw and feels burned from the outside in, but to his own amazement keeps going. Then his boxers fall down to his knees. He well-endowed and the veins in his penis bulging and pulsing with blood waiting to release its sperm, he lays down on the ground next to Tiffany.

The fucking feels so good to both of them, young love, sex----simple and barbaric at the same time. Tiffany looks at Victor, "oh no, don't come yet." She pulls out the garrote, "my turn." Just like that Victor snapped like a wild beast, "Is this what you want bitch?" He grabs the garrote and slides it around Tiffany's neck and pulls with all of his might. To Victor's amazement this turned him on even deeper and more fully and he started to fuck and strangle Tiffany at the same time, she said nothing the whole time. At one point, Victor thought he had heard a small snap, maybe, like a small wishbone or delicate bone breaking. It was Tiffany's Hyoid bone that snapped and disintegrated with the force of the garrote. He came in her anyway, in the end he gave her what she wanted. When it was over and Victor felt defeated, he rolled over and pulled Tiffany into his chest, knowing right then and there, she was dead.

The moonlight that looked down on them was all that bared witness to this act of violence and passion. A secret between the moon and them and nothing else living or breathing. That old Sycamore tree saw it all but would not bear witness. He knew Tiffany was dead and he held her for a long time, it was in those moments he knew that he had fallen in love with her and sobbed like a baby. With that realization, in a rush, in a panic, Victor buries the garrote under a big rock, and leaves Tiffany on the cold, dark, Connecticut ground and flees.

This brutal murder, as the town called it, was everywhere. Big news, and someone was going to pay for this act of violence. If this were all there was to night that Tiffany died, this would allow Victor to get away. But the cameras outside the Holly Oaks Country Club combined with Anna Davis's dreams have been able to put young Victor right where he desperately did not want to be, in the hands of the Farmington Police Department. Not to mention the garrote they found hidden under rock in the nearby woods had Victor's fingerprints and guilt all over it, an open and shut case; a dream case for the young, brazen, female assistant district attorney that was drooling all over it!

The warrant was issued, and Victor Guðmundsdóttirr was arrested the next day outside of Farmington. Twenty-three years old, without a clue, without a penny, without hope, void of anyone. Deer in the headlights of his own life.

The Police charged Victor with both murders as both girls' deaths involved garrots and hammers were the same. both murders, Tiffany Garrett, and Jenna Parker. If convicted, he would likely NOT get the death penalty as Connecticut does not have it in State. The Prosecutor and assistant DA were going to motion the Court to have the trial moved to Pennsylvania so they could seek the death the penalty. The Police believed he did kill all these girls in the same way, and because everyone else was void, they just had him. They wanted a conviction.

Connecticut and the small town of Farmington and their citizens, especially this privileged few at the Holly Oaks Country Club finally had their so-called justice for the girls, the Police had their suspect in custody and the world was going to sit better. Little did anyone know though, Victor accidently killed Tiffany at her urging mistakenly with the garotte but had nothing to do with the murders of the other girl but had an idea who did. He told this to the Police over and over again. That did not even matter now because Tom and Paul were gone, the Eurotrash Group was just gone. Everyone abandoned and dismantled after the murders just like his uncle and his friend did back then. Victor only remained, and it shall be him.

The media in town was going berserk, coverage on every channel, finding Victor guilty before the trial even began. People protesting, families and churches screaming burn him alive. No trial or lawyer could save Victor, he was found guilty the minute he was arrested and would pay the hefty price of his life for these girls and their lives lost. No questions asked, no other possibility considered; just guilty.

He lay now on a hard slab in a dimly lit hell hole waiting for his inevitabilities. Starving, cold, wet, and damp, laying in a puddle of his transgressions, missing home, and love. A hollow shell, his impending fate matters no more for he has already died.

Poor Victor, a sacrificial lamb for the slaughter of all iniquity and in that moment the blue azure water lends him his comfort.

Eddie.......

Inserted Chapter

You murderous people
who support a monster

It is all gone, Communist we are
Nothing for the people who implore, rotten to the core

My Cuba, Oh Cuba gone with the wind
Never helping us up with nothing to lend

You burned us at the stake and turned your back
Castro, Oh Castro, you are not coming back

Cuba is located where the northern Caribbean Sea, Atlantic Ocean, and Gulf of Mexico meet. It is an island nation surrounded by water. Havana is the capital of Cuba, an island country in the Caribbean Sea. It is the largest city in the Caribbean region. Havana is known for its many buildings from the time Cuba was a Spanish colony. The city lies on a bay with a protected harbor. The current population of Cuba in 2024 is 11,574,13 a 18% decline from 2023. The decline continues from the lack of appeal and has continued to decline over the years. Every year less and less. The island belongs mainly to those who were born there who still respect her and cherish her, protecting her from the world and her beauty unseen. The loyal natives, in fury with their land, born and breed, who survived the unspeakable before they were dead.

Castro's Cuba after the Bay of Pigs and the Cuban Missile Crisis

The failed invasion strengthened the position of Castro's administration, which proceeded to which openly supported the move towards socialism and the closer-knit ties with the Soviet Union, the disaster at the Bay of Pigs had a lasting impact on the Kennedy administration. Determined to make up for the failed invasion, the administration-initiated Operation Mongoose, a plan to destabilize and destroy the Cuban government and assassinate Fidel Castro.

Castro's government emphasized social projects to improve Cuba's standard of living, often to the detriment of economic development. Major emphasis was placed on education, and under the first 30 months of Castro's government, more classrooms were opened than in the previous 30 years.

After the revolution, the government of Fidel Castro managed to implement. successful health reform and growing job opportunities. These greatly benefited the population. Cuba also enjoyed a stable economy thanks to the support of the U.S.S.R.

As a Marxist–Leninist, Castro believed strongly in converting Cuba, and the wider world, from a capitalist system in which individuals own the means of production into a socialist system in which the means of production are owned by the workers.

The Cuban Revolution was known for equality. Under Castro, with the help of Soviet Union, for nearly 30 years Cuba was a stable socialist society. Between 1959 and December 1991 over 940,000 Cubans fled the Castro regime and entered the United States while Havana received massive subsidies from the Soviet Union. The Cuban exodus is the mass emigration of Cubans from the island of Cuba after the Cuban Revolution of 1959. Throughout the exodus, millions of Cubans from diverse social positions within Cuban society emigrated within various emigration waves, due to political suppression and disillusionment of life Cuba.

In October 1962, Kennedy decided to blockade Cuba and American forces were put on high alert. Kennedy addressed the American public and the world on television. He announced that there were Soviet missiles on Cuba and that the USA was blockading the island.

The Soviet Union had planted missiles in Cuba in direct alignment with striking the United States's major cities. The threat of the Soviets involvement with Castro panicked many Cubans and they are starting their exile then. The crisis was set off by the Soviet decision to station ballistic missiles in Cuba. Despite miscommunication and mixed messages, President John F. Kennedy and Soviet premier Nikita Khrushchev ultimately negotiated their way back from the brink of nuclear Armageddon. Crisis Averted.

Khruschev made it known that he was willing to withdraw his forces from Cuba if the United States agreed to never invade Cuba and to remove its missiles from Turkey. Kennedy was willing to accept, especially as those missiles were old and considered near obsolete.

The Bay of Pigs

President Kennedy cancelled a second air strike. On April 17, the Cuban-exile invasion force, known as Brigade 2506, landed at beaches along the Bay of Pigs and immediately came under heavy fire. Cuban planes strafed the invaders, sank two escort ships, and destroyed half of the exile's air support. The poor planning by Kennedy and the CIA along their underestimating of Castro's regime made the Bay of Pigs a failed disaster. Conditions in Cuba continue tenuous, and they were marching towards communism.

Eddie's parents Andoncia and Alejandro exiled from Cuba on a wooden boat they built in their community as thousands did, hoping it would be safe enough to conquer the one hundred miles of the Atlantic Ocean between Cuba and the Florida Keys. The raft was sturdy made from Indian Ebony and Diospyros, Eddie's family placed their sacred lives in the faith that this would wood or make shift vessel could sustain the Atlantic and get them to Florida where they could start a better life in a noncommunist country.

Eddie was only eight years old. It was 1976. He did not understand the implication of fleeing his homeland but knew that his family was in trepid danger and were risking all for the promise of freedom to come, that much even an eight-year-old could understand. His mom and dad had many talks with Eddie to prepare him for the exile when the day would come. They explained what the journey would entail to sail across the mighty Atlantic Ocean from Cuba to the Florida Keys. That could even be life threatening. They promised they would take every security measure they could and have every staple they could on board to ensure survival. This eased eight-year-old Eddie's mind. Eddie did not know any better but believed and trusted in his parents.

The rafts his community, friends, family, and neighbors were working on continuously would be the vessel in which they escaped. When the moment was right for the right family, they would be given the raft that was finished, and they would go next. It was a small knit community, probably only thirty people who were trying to exile alongside Eddie's family. They helped each other, cared for each other, and kept each other alive.

They fled Cuba at 1am and pushed off the Northern Coast towards the Florida Keys. They had planned, they had enough food and water for the two-day sail, plus clothes, blankets, and flashlights. The weather and water were calm upon departure and their spirits and hearts rang with pride.

If the weather continued to cooperate, they would be in the Florida Keys inside fifteen hours.

About five hours into the trip Eddie finally fell asleep. The dawn was breaking over the horizon, a new dawn speckled from within with the colors pink, orange, and red. Luminous and welcoming, we are going to make it his family chants. As my mother lulls me to sleep I dream of my America, I think about birthday parties, Halloween costumes, school, and friends; sunny days and the beach, my impending childhood to come as we approach Florida.

Florida Waters is a cool-toned deep blue color, reminiscent of the depths of the ocean. This versatile color works well with warm colors like coral and yellow

for a striking contrast or with neutrals for a more serene look. The color would bring a touch of the ocean to any design and would pair well with complementary colors such as sandy beige and seafoam green, luminous, magnificent, able to take three exiles and bring them forth home. Those cooling, welcoming waters of Florida. Blue Azure waters they were.

I am laying in my mother's loving arms, and just then, I am awakened from my dreaming with the thud under the raft. First like a small bump of a wave in the ocean, but then with a vigorous bump that nearly flips our small wooden cavity over. A nudge, a curiosity awakens both of my parents as the red hue dawn is nearing 8am.

The third thud knocked the raft into midair and when it smacked the water my father fell off into the water. I see him flailing about and my mother says swim. My father is now at the raft safely or so it seemed. When suddenly, he simply disappears beneath the blue, azure ocean waters. My mother and I never saw the shark, never even saw the fin, but after about three minutes of screaming for my dad, we did see a bloody, detached arm float up and hit the side of the raft. Our screams were only second to the knowledge that my father was gone and with our mouths left gasping for air, we simply allowed our spirits to die with him.

The blue azure water was so clear in those moments, I felt like I could see 100 feet down, and when I really looked, I could see my father smiling back to me at the surface, that blue azure water became my comfort----as it was my last memory of my father being alive and where he lost his life. It was at that moment that I let him go and carried that water with me for life.

Eddie and his mother made it to Key West eight hours later, with a vow from them both; small child and mother, that they were going to have great big full lives amidst their loss and never look back. It is what his father would have wanted. As they enter the United States after their exile from Cuba, they were forever changed and hated her already.

Anger resounds penetrating the skin. It can hide for years within our brain

as we live our lives robotically day to day. Until one day out of the blue we erupt. Our eruptions can be brief or last our lifetimes. They can be violent or just depressing, sometimes anger even takes on different forms; wherein we lose ourselves and become monsters. Especially those in repression, who forgot to grieve and who grew up becoming the boogeyman. It can happen to any of us. And just like that we are gone.

The Boogeyman is here, he can be found in any of us!

CHAPTER FIVE

Karen Scott

I play your game
But do it my way
You and I alone
Waiting for judgement day
I am captured, you are free
Take the next step to hear my plea
I didn't kill them, it wasn't me
Face me now so you can see

Anna

I finally am able to sleep now, after the devil left my bedside after he set my curtains on fire. I cleaned up the mess and threw my burnt curtains away. I will go to Walmart and buy new drapes, yes, that will cover all of this up. This space I am in right now, it's out of control, but in control, like I am meant to be here, there is something I am about to learn, maybe a deep dark secret about myself, about someone else.

I decided to call Lauren and ask her to come over and stay the night with me, for I am really afraid now. Afraid of me, my dreams, the devil, and my involvement in it all, I can't bear it alone, she comes right away.

We sit out on my small porch in front of my townhouse, which has a beautiful view of Holly Oaks and the 18th hole. One of the many perks of being an employee and member of the Club, great views and a bought lifestyle. I remember buying this townhome and feeling like I was on top of the world, all of my dreams were coming true, I had so much pride, but I am learning I took pride out of context, things for me are changing, I am changing.

Lauren brought over Chai tea, and I told her I would make it this time. I can walk without a limp now, and have begun PT. The OxyContin is now out of my body and mind, and I am moving in that respect.

I am not hopeful, even though the Police have a suspect in custody, all of these nightmares may be completely over for me, but not for Victor. His path will hell on earth, until there is no life anymore and he goes away forever.

I long for the day that I can actually focus on my therapy and maybe even go back to work to playing tennis again, normalcy. Sara called me yesterday and asked about my progress and I had to tell her I had a small setback----no one needs to know what that fully means. She tells me that her Varsity tennis team won an in-house tournament last week and that she was the star, she also told me that she had gotten her letter in tennis. She thanked me, and it felt so good to hear that something in my life is going well. Her picture would forever be on that wall in her high school gym.

Lauren meets me in the kitchen and asks what I want for dinner. I am hungry so we both jump in and make pasta with frozen meatballs, marinara and a green salad. After we eat, Lauren says she has work to do on her laptop and I make my way upstairs for a shower and early bed. "I am going to read a bit," I say. "Let me know if you need anything," says Lauren.

As I ascend the staircase, I look back down at Lauren at my dining room table working way in Lauren fashion, she looks up at me and just nods, and I suddenly know everything will be ok.

After my shower, I slip into my favorite Ann Taylor Pajamas, emerald, green with cheetahs on them and crawl into bed. I noticed the time, it is 9:15 and I am tired. I turn out my lamp and just allow myself to drift, to be free, unaware of what will come to me in my dreams, untethered and unbothered.

But I am dreaming now and struggling for the light to see for what I am dreaming to come into focus. I am waiting, all is quiet. I am back in the blue azure water now, I am drowning, I feel my lungs fill up with CO_2 as I gasp to breathe, I am screaming for help, as no one can hear me, I simply just let go and now I am floating. I see a young woman now, she is different from the other girls I have dreamt about, maybe older, more mature definitely, and not as pretty. She is wearing a business suit, yes, she seems to be in a meeting of some kind. A man stands up and shakes her hand, introducing himself and saying, "Welcome Ms., Scott." Yes, this woman is Karen Scott and she is about to graduate Dartmouth and is applying for jobs. She is happy and confident, as a young woman should be. She is going to get this job, I can just tell, my dreams don't lie.

I am somewhere else enow, someplace dark and cold with no affection just filled with antipathy and regret. I am inside of a jail cell and the only other person in there with me is a young man with European features and sunken in shoulders. A guard jingles his keys and opens the lock to his cell. "Your court-appointed attorney is here." The silhouette of a young man just scoots out of the cell and walks down a long dark corridor to a sullen room with no furniture just a table and a bench. The lawyer walks in and tells the young man that is facing two counts of capital murder and the prosecutor is asking for the death penalty. "It is an open and shut case," he says. "The evidence is here; you will be found guilty." The lawyer asks the silhouette to sign some papers and the silhouette replies, "I didn't do this, I am innocent." The lawyer just shakes his head and checks his watch. "It is late, just think about things over night, if you take this plea, your situation will be somewhat better." "You will still probably receive the death penalty, but maybe be able to live longer, have better accommodations, just think about, would you?" "The prosecution is seeking a change of venue to Pennsylvania where they can seek the death penalty and the judge may grant it considering the murders were widespread, meaning not committed in the same counties." "If that happens you will get the death penalty, if the judge denies a change of venue, even with the plea bargain, you could just get a reduced life sentence." With that the lawyer just leaves and the guard is back in the room and escorts the silhouette back to the tiny cell.

The silhouette is crying now and then praying, praying to the same God we all do hoping for the answers and the forgiveness. The silhouette turns his face upward to the ceiling and I know in that moment in this dream that silhouette is Victor. He needs my help and he needs a proper defense attorney and immediately I think of Ed Garcia.

Victor's thoughts became transparent to me in these moments, and I know that he did kill Tiffany Garrett by accident when their choking game went too far, but he did not kill Jenna Parker or Elise Frank or anyone else for that matter, even though he stands accused. Then who did? Why aren't the Police looking into this more closely and with more care? I know, because they have got Victor, and this town wants a murder conviction. Victor has admitted to the death he caused on Tiffany Garrett, after that, the Police did not want to hear anything Victor had to say. Victor was the man, that was it, guilty and no chance of being proven innocent. No one cared about the accused, only the victims and that they were dead.

All of a sudden, I can't breathe, and I am choking, my head pops out of the blue azure water only for a moment, then takes me under again. The tide is pulling me towards, towards, towards something, the truth.

I am thinking of Victor again, and how they can arrest him and lock him up with no hard evidence, even with no regard to Tiffany's murder. There has to be something legal that can be done, something to prove his innocence. The law is too tricky and the lines of what is evidence and not, can often times be blurred. An innocent human life is on the line, I have been pulled into this now, I may be his only hope.

The Quantum evidence or simply quantum is the amount of evidence needed, the quality of proof is how dependable such evidence should be considered. On the other hand, quantum of evidence means that how much evidence will be given in particular cases. Quantum of evidence solely based on the quality of all evidence that will be provided in a particular case: Can a person be convicted on testimony alone? Yes. The law in virtually every state is well settled that the testimony even of a single witness, if believed, is sufficient to support a conviction. End of story.

The "corpus delecti" rule, which is the law in some jurisdictions but not necessarily in all, provides that a defendant's own confession cannot support a conviction standing alone, but there must in addition be some independent evidence that a criminal act was committed. That additional evidence, of course, can be witness testimony.

There is no requirement that there be some kind of physical evidence in order for the prosecution to obtain a conviction or to meet its burden of proof beyond a reasonable doubt, that is, shall we say, an urban myth. Prisons are full of people convicted on the basis of witness testimony only. It sounds as though you are seriously misunderstanding whatever is in your book . . . or that your book got it wrong.

I am back in his cell now; he is crying and his back lurched up like an animal, unable to feel or comprehend. There are cockroaches in his cell, working their way from the small dime size hole in the wall of his cell and marching in a straight line toward him. Victor tries to close his eyes and pretend this happening to him, he came here from Iceland for a chance at a good life, a better life, a family, maybe even a house. He left Iceland to find that here, first in Maine and then in Connecticut, he felt betrayed, deep down from being born with little opportunity, to the time when his uncle and his friend ran away to ever getting involved with the Eurotrash at the Club, but one thing he had no regrets about was Tiffany. He loved her, just a little too late and little too hard.

These United States had failed him, taken away his barren hopes and dreams. He made a poor decision to take up with the young men at the Club; "Eurotrash." He just wanted friends and a path, a life of some sort but suddenly got caught up in someone else's mess. He didn't kill Jenna Parker, who knows who killed these other girls? Because he accidently killed Tiffany Garrett and they had his semen in her,

73

and his prints on the garrote, they can find him guilty of killing Jenna Parker too, connected homicides you see----both sexual acts before brutal means of murder. A real serial killer is what the Police called him. This is where the Police are going! The Quantam proof is enough, they do not need anything else, they have two witness' from the Club identifying Victor as being seen with Tiffany and the other girls on several occasions and the camera on the back deck of the Club puts him at the murder scene that night. But I know he didn't do it, he knows he didn't do it, but then who, who is responsible, who could commit these heinous, random acts of violence, or were they even random at all? Maybe this murderer was hardwired from the time he was a child.

He is now curled up in a ball on his firm cot, in the fetal position, with no one to believe him but me. "I am here Victor it is me Anna, I believe you and I will help you, somehow, let it be me!"

Karen Scott did get the job, she found out the next day. The first person she called was her mother and the second a financer out of New York City, her new boyfriend, Jason Wentworth, who is ten years older but already made his fortune at 32. He was looking for a trophy wife, and Karen was the one for him.

Karen Scott could be a trophy wife, but also, she just accepted a job at Langston, Hughes, and Scott as Paralegal, before starting law school in the fall. Langston, Hughes, and Scott were the big fish law firm in Farmington, Connecticut and her father Brad Scott was one of the founding partners. Karen Scott and her father knew a lot about Quantum of Evidence and Corpus Delecti. This was the firm's specialty being able to get their desired verdict by manipulating the evidence in either direction, even without concrete proof, thus making the firm's notoriety infamous and those who work there, Gods.

Karen was the envy of all who lived in Farmington and especially those who were part of Holly Oaks, she was our poster child for all good things. I toss and turn in my sleep, Karen Scott is such a big presence in my dream, but why?

I am back in that cell with Victor, he is praying again asking for God to spare him these charges for these unjust accusations and crimes. He never even wanted to be part of "Eurotrash" or play the choking games, he just wanted better. He never meant to kill Tiffany Garrett or even harm her for that matter, he liked her, had a crush on her---grew to love her. It was the heat of the moment, her begging and the vodka that made him get carried away with it all and pull the garrote too tight around her neck, a moment he will always regret.

"Tighter and tighter," she screamed, were Tiffany's last words to him. She wanted it up until the very end. He cries now and lays back on his cold, concrete slab acting as a makeshift bed. I wish I could comfort him now, soothe away his pain, but I know I can't. So, I leave him there in my dream alone and abandoned singing my witching hours lullaby to him.

I am back in my different dream now with Karen Scott, she is at a party, in a red dress with her long curly blonde hair cascading down her back. She is smiling, but I sense trouble, maybe even danger looming in that room. Where, where where is she? Then my dream became vivid and I knew she is standing in the ballroom at The Holly Oaks Country Club. This is a party for her firm and her boyfriend is there, he has his hand in the small of her back, which is bare. She has gone now in the ladies' room putting in her red lipstick to match her party dress. Then she is, she is just gone. She had vanished. I blink rapidly in my sleep, where did she go, where did she go?

I see again in my dream she is outside smoking a cigarette, (I didn't know she smoked), with a young European looking man, I have seen him before at the Club it is some, I think I know, definitely not Victor though.

She is walking in front of him now and they are laughing heading out towards the woods where Tiffany Garrett lost her life and two other girls had been before and know all too well, that is where the choking game took place.

"Oh My God," Oh I cry I am tossing and turning and burning up with fever in my bed. "He is going to kill her; he is going to kill." "Run Karen, Run!"

Just then I snap up in my bed and know that the killer is not Victor, "They are going to burn an innocent man, they are going to burn an innocent man!" It is just intuition or premonition, I have no proof, but I just know, Victor is innocent.

And with that knowledge I dial Officer Pell's number as Lauren storms in my room. "I need help Lauren, I need help." "I have got you," she says, and holds me until the Police arrive back at my house. "It will be ok Anna; it will be ok." "Just breathe." The blue azure water is comforting me with all of her pressure and volatility, making it hard not to relax. I put my head on my best friend's shoulder and disappeared into a passive state of acknowledgement.

The blue and red lights of the Police cars have become the beckon lights of my Holly Oaks neighborhood, filled with hope and the way home.

CHAPTER SIX

Dreamscapes

Lullaby sweet lullaby
The stars, the moon, the sky is sleeping
Lullaby, oh Lullaby
The Devil comes creeping

Escapism into a surrealistic scene is the foreshadow and backdrop of my own reality. My dreamscape now is where I find the answers, the answers about my own peril and life and about the death of those three girls. I have decided to be hypnotized to see if there is anything here that can be helpful to the Police, something I may be suppressing something I have forgotten or never even known.

I am being hypnotized on Thursday by Dr. Samantha Gibbs at her office at the Central CT Hospital in Hartford. I have read all of the pamphlets and materials and signed all of the consent forms; I am ready and I have learned a lot.

Hypnosis, also referred to as hypnotherapy or hypnotic suggestion, is a trance-like state in which you have heightened focus and concentration. Hypnosis is usually done with the help of a therapist using verbal repetition and mental images. When you're under hypnosis, you usually feel calm and relaxed, and are more open to suggestions.

Hypnosis can be used to help you gain control over undesired behaviors or to help you cope better with anxiety or pain or in some instances help you regain memory or suppressed trauma, like sexual abuse, or a violent act.

It's important to know that although you're more open to suggestion during hypnosis, you don't lose control over your behavior.

Today is the day. Lauren, Ed Garcia, and I arrive ahead of the Police at the office of Samantha Gibbs, M.D. Doctor of Psychiatry. She was referred to me by Officer Pell and the Farmington Police Department as a whole, she is widely used in many cases and practices hypnosis weekly, the Police Force knows her well and works with her often.

She, in and of herself, casts quite a spell, surprisingly, she is fit and very attractive almost in a movie star way maybe this was part of her allure for hypnosis.

Her office is very sedative and calming, a place any person would love to be almost like an oasis but that is just the point. Pink and muted red artwork on the wall, abstract so that you feel swept away into the paintings, beige leather furniture and off-white puffy carpet. There is a small waterfall built into the wall adjacent to her desk, which is Mahogany, grand and feminine at the same time.

After all of the introductions are made, Dr Gibbs asked who would be staying, the less people in the room the better.

I immediately asked Lauren to stay for moral support and Officer Pell demanded that he stay for legal reasons then Ed Garcia chimed in citing the same reason. It was decided all would stay, but Dr. Gibbs made it completely clear that she was in charge and that no one was allowed to speak or comment or even cough during the hypnosis. "We all wanted same thing here, the truth." "The only chance that we have is to let the hypnosis happen in a completely organic and transparent way, void of any interruption." "You have to the let the process simply unfold." We all agreed. "let's begin," she said. Dr. Gibbs begins, she starts the same way every time:

- Ask permission to begin the process of hypnotic induction.
- Follow Marisa Peer's Rapid Eye Movement technique. Ask the client to close their eyes and roll up their eyes. Look out for the moment the eyes flicker under your client's eyelids.
- Focus on deepening your client's trance. For example, repeat relaxing phrases in a smooth, melodic voice.
- Ensure this process is not rushed.
- Learn how to recognize the subtle signs of someone in a trance.

As the hypnosis begins, I hear her voice, sweet but sharp, kind but on purpose. Almost like she is directing me in a movie, telling me where to go, what to do, until it is just me. "Deeper and deeper into the warm water, let yourself go inch by inch." Dr. Gibbs continues, until I am somewhere unaware of myself, but somewhere safe. I am back now in the blue azure water, floating through ripples of her silky waves; she is my truth serum.

"Anna, can you hear me now?" "Yes," I answer. "Good, now tell me what you see?"

Me:

"I see me, I am at the Holly Oaks Country Club in my tennis outfit." I had just finished a tennis lesson with Sara Rainer and was talking with my friend Eddie, the Club's groundskeeper.

Eddie was telling me about how beautiful he thought Sara was, and all of the girls actually here at the Club. He had a thing for the young "Country Club" girls, it used to creep me out a bit when he spoke like that, but I would let it roll off, claiming that is just Eddie. He was a bit of a flirt, especially with the young girls------- but loved women, these women of Holly Oaks, but then who didn't? No one really suspects about Eddie, just a horndog like every other man.

I loved my job and being there at the Club, I was proud, in my place, right where I belonged, this was as close to celebrity as I would get. I had a career, a home, friends, stature, and positioning, I had a good life, I was happy. "Why am I here then?"

I see Lauren now, she is coming into the Club in her new Gucci blazer and Valentino shoes, she is laughing with her husband, rich and boastful, just like it should be here at Holly Oaks Country Club, perfection magnified, happiness sold separately. "That is Lauren." Even though Al and Lauren didn't have a traditional marriage, they were happy even though they tried like hell to hide it sometimes. I loved the sense of seeing Lauren, always have. I would do anything for her, she would do anything for me.

Then there is a sadness to her. She is sad at the Club sometimes, I can not put my finger on it, it just is something I sense. I see Al now, Lauren's husband, he is ogling one of the young daughters of a prestigious member then another girl, right behind Lauren's back. These girls were special though, everyone looked at them.

I am drifting again, this time into the ballroom and I see many different people, handsome men, but the women Oh, how beautiful and privileged they were, just like real princesses. Their gowns, hair, make up and cleavage, Oh My! I never was jealous of these young women, but I knew a lot of the Country Club women hated them. The wives of handsome successful men, doctors, lawyers, congressmen; and they were mid-fifties and trying everything to keep themselves up, but gravity and time were winning that race. These women felt impotent, like losers and they knew what their husbands really liked. These Holly Oaks women felt scorned by time and reality, even all the money in the world couldn't deny their age and they had hated it. They wanted the one thing they simply couldn't have or buy: youth.

These husbands paid attention to the young women, who didn't? Lauren could be jealous of the young at the Club, always bitching about them, licentious and full of sex, wanting to get their claws into their future, full bosoms and filled with an eagerness to please. And these men; their victims. Yes, Holly Oaks could be a regular Peyton Place sometimes. Oh, the secrets she holds. Husbands cheated, and everyone turned a blind eye.

I drift and shift again; I am in the kitchen at the Club now and the staff leaves the back door open for ventilation sometimes when the weather is cool. I can see out of the back door and lead to a large patio the just beyond the woods and the marina. Staff hang out there sometimes before or after work or even during their shifts to take a quick 10-minute break or smoke a cigarette.

I see Victor now, he is jolly and singing, helping by filling the plates for the cook and putting them under the heating lamps. "Pick up for table one," I hear another young waiter yell. He is also European. I heard someone call him Darrs? They were all talking about a co-worker named Cedric who hit the jackpot with a much older widow at the Club and was moving in with her. He had quit the kitchen relieved of his duties in his abandonment for better. He had already received several thousand dollars from her, all for just fucking her and she likes to fuck, they were saying how Cedric had to eat her pussy every day in the morning, before she even washed, Darrs almost dropped his plate of food, there has to be an easier way to make it then to have to eat fifty-two-year-old beaver. "You all are just jealous," Cedric would say, "all I have to do is eat her pussy once a day and fuck her whenever she wants and I get paid!" "I live in the lap of luxury, I made it, I won the game!" "What man does not like to fuck even the ugly or old ones."

It is dark now; I am back outside again and the patio and woods intrigue me so I stay right there. The sight of the marina in the distance, lonely, sterile, not busy, because it is nighttime. It is dark at the marina, not many lights and many, many trees.

This marina holds a secret, these woods won't tell it, the ground lay dormant, spoiled by it. Secrets are here, souls are here, murdered girls are here. "I sense something wicked here," I shout. I am tossing and turning in the chair. "Should we wake her up now," asks Ed?

"Not now, not yet" says Dr. Gibbs, "let's go deeper."

ME: Through Tiffany

I am somewhere else now. I am at a cotillion or debutante ball. A very special event indeed, black tie and ballgowns and the most beautiful faces you have ever seen. In the United States this is a formal presentation of young women, débutantes, to " polite society ", typically hosted by a charity or society. Those introduced can vary from the ages of 16 to 18 (younger ages are more typical of Southern regions, while older are more commonplace in the North). The debutante here is Tiffany Garrett and her dad is walking her across the stage. Her dad, Matthew Garrett, is a lawyer, and was recently elected to Congress as our Junior Representative. He was a big deal, but in this moment with his daughter, nothing else mattered, except her.

What no one knows about Tiffany is even though she was a debutant and a crown jewel, she had been having sexual relations since she was thirteen. She had sex at thirteen and lost her virginity with the captain of the football team on the Varsity Team in high school, Danny Miller, he was seventeen and an a junior. After him, when she was fifteen, she was having an affair with a man of twenty-five who worked at a grocery store in Farmington, two miles from where she lived. His name was Diego and she really thought she could have loved him, maybe her first love, but later found out he was hooking up with any woman at the grocery store or around town. Tiffany felt used, but at the same time one of the girls, she liked sex and was not ashamed about it. When Tiffany was sixteen, she met a man at the mall. He was so good looking and tall and well groomed. His name was Jack and this time her lover was forty and married. They met always on Friday nights at his house when his wife was at her girl's night out. They had illicit sex and he even plied Tiffany with wine some nights. It was on the last occasion that that they were together that right in the middle of their love making, he pulled out a silk stash and wrapped it around her neck, tighter and tighter. She was so scared that this time, she had gotten in too deep, and that Jack was going to kill her. In the last seconds before she thought she may have stopped breathing, he released. He bent over and kissed her deep and touched her in a way that made her have her first orgasm, and with all of that, Tiffany fell in love.

Her family never knew any of this. Tiffany was their pride and joy. This is her secret life, private from her image and parents and her parents were image people.

Matt had worked his whole life to serve the great state of Connecticut. Tiffany was an only child and Matthew and Gayle Garrett spent all of their time on her, had the highest the expectations for her and loved her dearly. Tiffany was now just eighteen, just turned eighteen, on the cusp of her life. She didn't have a boyfriend at the time, but rumor at the Club was that she was heavily infatuated with the new bus boy from Iceland, Victor Guðmundsdóttirr. Rumor has it, they had been on a few dates, and he loved her. The Eurotrash group that worked at the Club though was like family to him since he had no one here in the United States of his own, his allegiance was there to them, they feed him, they employed him, they housed him, they loved him in that suto European way of being nonchalant.

Since Cedric quit, and moved in with Rose Hildenbrandt, that left a vacancy that Victor filled. Darrs, who was their leader, got fired for stealing 100.00 from the cash register one night at work. So that left Victor, Paul, and Tom. They formed a solid union calling themselves the three Euroketters, but the members of the Club referred to them as Eurotrash. They were after a group of young girls at the Club, Tiffany was one of them that looked perfect like a doll on the outside but had a funky side behind the designer gowns.

These men were known as slimy con artists and were known trouble at the Club.

These girls of their choice were Tiffany Garrett, Jenna Parker, Elise Frank, and Karen Scott. These men had their sights on these four women. The night Tiffany died, Jenna and Elise met Paul and Tom at the Club. Because there were only three men and four women, Karen Scott was quaza eliminated, everyone just paired up. Paul, Jenna, Tom, and Elise and of course Victor and Tiffany. For Karen's sake, luckily, she never fit in. No one seemed upset, it was what it was, three men: three women. Karen never got involved any deeper with any of them. She had bigger fish to fry and was laser focused on her future.

They all met in the Club's kitchen because they had the keys, being kitchen employees and wanted more stocked opportunity for the young to party. Food and liquor at their disposal.

They entered the kitchen that night quietly, but then started to get extremely rowdy. Paul turned on some music and the girls were drinking Jack Daniels and Grey Goose out of the bottles, straight. They were already intoxicated, slurring their words, and screaming obscenities. These girls wanted it, they had party on their minds, maybe because all of them were prodigies in some way, maybe they felt too sheltered, but here at the Club, they were free.

Jenna took her top off and then her bra and sat topless on top of the kitchen counter while Paul cut pieces of salami and threw them into her mouth like a game. He took a big pull off a nearly empty Grey Goose bottle and then he started fondling her breasts after he took a big bite of salami and put it in Jenna's mouth and kissed her.

Elise loosened her spaghetti straps and let her dress hit the floor and was wearing nothing but thong undies. Jenna started kissing Paul and his was rubbing her breasts then licking them, when Jenna, out of nowhere, clasped her small hand around his throat. She choked him until he couldn't take it anymore, his face seethed with anger and sexual pleasure, both.

"What are you doing, I couldn't breathe." When he finished gasping for air, he threw her face down on the counter, with a loud thud, and nearly raped her, and it would have been rape, if Jenna didn't beg for it. He was so angry but energized and charged at the same time. Tiffany and Victor laughed and walked out of the back of the kitchen onto the deck holding hands, walking out into the moonlight towards the marina lake and the woods.

What seemed like only moments later, Paul, Tom, Elise, and Jenna joined, but disappeared into the woods, leaving Tiffany and Victor alone, and no one saw what happened next, except the moon and the evil of the night. No one saw what really happened, no one got to see Victor fall in love with Tiffany. No one got to see how it really happened. The garrote he pulled too tight, stole me in the night air.

What a shameless waste, my life is gone now. I know that Victor did not mean to hurt me, it was a game, and he would do anything to please me. We were falling in love and would never hurt one another. My death was an accident, and no one should be blamed except for me for wanting to play the game and my putting him in the position of he had to. The garrot was all me, my doing. To be strangled gave me pleasure just like Jack had taught me a couple of years ago. I thought it would go the same as it did back then, but I didn't. Too much of a good thing can really be too much.

I would never really know what true love means, for I am dead now. I really didn't get to know.

I was stupid, but I wanted to feel, I wanted to be, I wanted too much, things my parents tried to give me, but couldn't.

Things I will never have.....

The woods behind the Holly Oak Country Club where Tiffany Garrett died.

ME: Through Jenna

Jenna Nicole Parker was a beauty right from the start. Her parents knew it by the time she was three years old. I mean the type of beauty only bestowed on a few of us. By the time Jenna was five years old her parents realized that she could sing, the voice of an angel her family called it. A gift bestowed by God and exploited by her parents. By the time Jenna was six her mother had enrolled her in every pageant Statewide and Nationwide. She won her first beauty pageant at the age of seven years old and never stopped winning, that was who she was, who she became. A beauty pageant queen in the making, everyone's perfect doll.

As Jenna aged, the life of a beauty pageant winner was taxing. A teenage girl wanted certain things, French fries, soda, pizza, and boys. Beauty pageant life was anything, if not disciplined.

Most days Jenna was fine with it, but some days, the really hard days she would just sit and cry, nothing else really to do to comfort herself. By the time she hit high school, she was almost considered weird by her peers, to some that were in her close circle though, a legend in the making. When Jenna won the Miss Connecticut Teen pageant, her status was even elevated by those who worshipped her. Her future plans were to compete in Miss America and obtain scholarship money for college, maybe Yale, where she wanted to study medicine.

Jenna was anything but perfect, she had a secret she had been hiding for years, if not her whole lifetime. In order to maintain her path in the pageant world and now qualify for Miss America, she had to stay within a certain weight class for her height. No one ever knew, but Jenna was bulimic. She had been on and off her whole life. The binges gave her treats that she mentally thought she needed and in those few moments she did. She felt like she was not missing out on her favorite foods, the ones everyone else got to eat. The purging gave her the control she thought she needed. She was obsessed, caught between this world of having her cake and eating too and the world of always having to perfect, impossible to maintain. Her dreams were her dreams and she was going to do anything and everything she could to achieve them.

Those dreams were cut short, the night she was left to be burned in the barn off the Old Highway by someone the Police had no clue who it is. They think it is Victor, after all he did kill Tiffany, but they are wrong, dead wrong.

Poor Jenna dead, but no justice, dead, but still very much alive to those who loved her.

The night it happened I was on my way to the market to buy ingredients for a new recipe of brownies I saw online. My plan was to make them, and then eat the whole pan and pueke my insides out. Something Jenna was good at.

I am not sure what even happened to me, but what I do remember is right before I died smoke had invaded my lungs and permeated my being, finding it impossible to draw breath. I smelled cinder and soot and could see the red flames dancing in front of my face about to be caught up in them, one with them.

I never saw my killer, but know I was bludgeoned and left here to burn. He crept up on me and took me by surprise, I could feel his rage by the way the object struck my head, sharp, splitting my scalp and matter seeping out. My bag of brownie ingredients spilling on the ground. My poor brownies was my last thought before I became unconscious.

I am gasping my final breaths of oxygen muddled in smoke when those horses just stood there, useless, they couldn't get out either and they couldn't help me, it was fated.

I just died a meaningless death in a burning down barn with two horses who gasped and begged for their lives even more than I did, silly species, silly horses, doomed to die and too stupid to know it.

Burning to death in a barn with my two horses gave me the comfort I needed until I made my eternal escape into the blackness that now holds me dear.

The barn where Jenna Parker died and burned.

ME: Through Elise:

I feel like I am back at the lake now, I can hear voices around me in the room, I think I hear Dr. Gibbs, but then I am transported back into my vegetive state of hypnosis and begin to break the barriers of what is really happening and trying to get out. My dreamscape is thin, dissipating, but I am still here.

I am in her life now, her thoughts, her happenings, Elise Frank, who was she, and what happened to her?

Richard Ellis Frank was Farmington Connecticut Gold, the big Fish! He was the richest man by far in Farmington and more importantly at the Club. He was a collector of old cars and antiquities and had the biggest house in Holly Oaks. He has two sons, and one daughter Elise.

His two sons were just one and a half years apart and both handsome, smart, well accomplished men. One had just graduated from Stanford and the other just accepted at Yale. Then there was Elise, you know you hear the term "Daddy's Girl all of the time, well Elsie was anything but." Elise was salubrious and bland in her looks, but not completely ugly, but her appearance didn't warm her father's heart and she felt it. Her mother Nancy Frank came from money and good breading and did her best with Elise. Fancy dress, County Club, the best education and friends, social status, and breeding. Elise Frank had a very nice pedigree, but she was sad, felt the disappointment of her father and her mother for being ordinary and she began to withdraw.

After some time of being withdrawn, she became rebellious and started hanging out with undesirable people behind her parents' back, maybe in a form of rebellion, or to find herself or maybe just wanted to have fun.

Before she got involved with the Eurotrash at the Club, she had been seeing one of the Black valet car attendants, Darryl Jones. He was poor, but bright and hard working. The kind of man that her parents would never have approved of.

After seeing each other for four months, on the down low, Elise found out she was pregnant. When she confronted Darryl, he skipped out on her and would not have anything to do with her anymore or that unborn baby. Elise had nowhere to go and no one to turn to.

She saw a commercial for an abortion clinic in Hartford, just about twenty minutes away and went in for a consult. But because she was not eighteen needed a parental consent. Elise, in that moment, felt so helpless and trapped.

There were many times over he next two weeks that Elise tried to talk to her parent about the pregnancy but every time couldn't do it.

Out of sheer desperation Elise decided to take matters into her own hands and end the pregnancy.

The day she killed her unborn child, she broke into her parent's liquor cabinet and drank as much Maker's Mark as she could stand. She then stripped down and climbed into her bathtub. She spread her longs so far apart that a grizzly bear could have fucked her. She took the end of a manipulated wire clothes hanger and plunged it deep into her cervix and then her uterus. Blood became the bathtub and it hurt.

When she could see no more white of the tub she knew she had succeeded. The bright red blood allowed for the chunks of the baby to float in it, giving its life no meaning.

In these moments Elise disappeared forever.

Elise met Paul, Tom, and Victor at the Club one late afternoon and Victor set out the water glasses and linens for dinner. Victor introduced her to both Paul and Tom and Elise became infatuated with Paul, but Paul was already into Jenna, so she turned her attention and prowess on Tom. He was rough in look and demeaner and came across like James Dean in a Rebel Without a Cause, her favorite movie. They started texting and sexting and they became involved, she would see Tom on the down low, unbeknownst to her parents or anybody for that matter, her secret, her life. The first night she fucked him was ten days after they met, and the sexting would no longer suffice. The longing and lust became too much for them both. She fucked him often from that point forward and he made her feel beautiful, made her feel that she was special, a feeling Elise needed to feel for a very long time, if ever. Elise and Tom were falling in love. She never got to tell Tom, but though she may have been pregnant, the cheap drug store pregnancy test only cost $9.99, but she was determined to take it. Intuitive little Elise, she was pregnant and the time of her death when someone slashed her throat all the back to her spinal cord. A partial decapitation of the making. Even nearly headless, in her final moments of life she knew who he was, what he had done, but she would not be there to tell it. She knew the murderer.

I like this dream; I like where I am at----this information is coming to me. Then suddenly I am pulled into a storm of dark clouds and wicked winds, what is happening now? I am twisting and turning. I see a knife, the knife that slit Elise's throat, the throat slit that Victor is being blamed for, but he didn't do it, I know he didn't, the person in my dream now is walking toward Elise with the big knife. They are near the pavilion with the marina, the same one where her body was found. I can't make anything else out, is it Paul? Did Paul do this heinous act, I don't know, but I don't feel like he did it. I am rolling and trying to solve this puzzle, when, I think I can see him, is it, is it?

The thunder rolls and the lightning strikes and I am struck by the lightning and for a moment; all goes black.

The marina where Elise Frank lost her life by way of partial decapitation.

Me: Through Karen

I am feeling woozy now, not like in a drunk way, but like someone gave me a shot of midazolam. I am still in hypnoses, painting like a dog, I may have even turned into a dog. I bark, "Ruff, ruff." Hear me, help me, believe me.

Karen was going to be his next mark, his next victim. This killer moved in a very particular but predictable pattern. I dreamed this at my home in Holly Oaks. The Police have taken me seriously now and alerted Karen. She is on the lookout and taking extreme precautions during this time when a potential serial killer is on the loose in our town. She is smart enough to realize that this killer has a pattern and that there is someone who is hunting and murdering girls in this town in a very precise way.

I heard through rumors that Karen was even getting ready to leave the state and stay with family elsewhere until the killer had been found. Good for her, get out while she can.

Whoever was killing these girls, was it the same person? They wanted Karen Scott next, why? I am tossing and turning over on myself and can see something coming right at me like an arrow. This murderer is a collector; Jenna Parker, pageant Queen, Elise Frank, the riches of the rich and now Karen Scott an independent, ivy league educated woman on her way to becoming a lawyer. He didn't adore these women, he hated them! He wanted their heads on a pike. Something inside of him or something that happened to him made him hate women. The mere thought of a successful or beautiful woman had to stopped, wiped away from the face of this earth. It was the way he killed the women; Jenna was beat and burnt, and Elie's throat slit so far back that she was almost beheaded. He wanted Karen Scott, but with Office Pell's help he would never get a shot at her. I was able to save one life, one life indeed, the wonder of the beautiful Karen Scott and her lovely, big future.

I am turning again and sweating through my clothes, my breathing is shallow and I can't get enough air in. I hear Dr. Gibbs, "Just a few more minutes." Everything goes black again and I am in blue azure water, knee deep.

I am flailing now in the blue azure water now just like when I was six years old and fell of a boat on a family vacation. It is hard to breathe, I am gasping for air, why is this happening to me? Right before I go under, I see my best friend Lauren mouth the words, "Let Go and keep quiet."

Me: Through Eddie

I am somewhere else now. I am about to go back under the water when my old friend from the Club comes into my dream. "Eddie, is that you"?

Eddie was in a bowling league, besides taking care of, and doing a wonderful job at, keeping the grounds at the Club, this was his life.

He never married or had any children but had many friends through the Club in all of his years employed, I, being his best friend. Many days after work, Eddie and I would sit on the veranda at the Club and sip peach iced tea or even Bloody Mary's. We would gossip about the members and we would always sit and look at the green, the perfectly manicured lawn and trees, bushes, and flowers; his pride and joy; his purpose. His Crepe Myrtles that he showed extra care to were always his favorites.

He lived on Holly Oak Country Club property. The Management had gifted Eddie, through his employment, a small guest house in back of the main house, only about 1000 square feet, but I had been in there many times and Eddie had kept a beautiful little home, nothing out of place. Everyone loved Eddie. His property was lined with the most beautiful magenta colored Crepe Myrtle trees, he loved those trees and every night they welcomed him home. Crepe Myrtles, he often referred to as God's gift to him.

I am tossing and turning again, I am back in the blue azure water, when I was six years old again, I can't breathe.

I snap back to Eddie's house now, but then I see a tarp and can almost see under it. It is a big tarp, lying on Eddie's living room floor. Why does he have a trap in his living room? His house was always so orderly and in order.

I am almost ready to wake, I can hear Dr. Gibbs and Lauren's voices, "One more minute, one more question." "Anna, what do you see in Eddie's house what is it,

Anna?" "I can see from his living room window, the crepe myrtles in their bright pink color, showing off for Eddie, they adore him"" "What else Anna, come on."

I am back in Eddie's house now in the front room where he watches TV, back to the tarp. I see, I see under it and there are two cans of gasoline, burnt dirty clothes and a pair of rubber boots. There is also a bloody knife stuffed into a plastic baggie, the baggie is too small I see the point of the knife piercing the bag and jetting out. I SEE WHAT LOOKS LIKE A HUMAN BODY, of a young slender man or a woman, I cannot tell. I hear someone speak it is a woman's voice though. It sounds like, so familiar to me, could it be, it is the voice of my best friend Lauren, why is she here, she barely knew Eddie and why was she in this vision with the tarp? She says, "Let us get this body out of here." Is this true, I can't make sense of any of this.

I am back in my childhood now, to when I was six years old, and I fell off a boat and almost drowned. The blue azure water was calming me as I let go and stopped breathing, in that second all was calm all was ok, even when little body went limp. The most traumatizing thing that ever happened to me until this moment.

"Help me," I cry, "Get me out of here!" "Her blood pressure is way too high I am going bring her out," says Dr. Gibbs. "Anna, listen to my voice when I count to ten, you will be fully awake and back in this room with us." I listen with full all heedfulness to Dr. Gibbs counting. "Five, six, seven." I am now back in the room and looking at all of the people who witnesses this hypnosis.

My eyes scan the room, blinking and darting. When I know that I am safe, I draw in a deep breath and simply cry.

Lauren

I am awake now and drinking water sitting on Dr. Gibbs' couch. "We have made great progress Anna" says Dr. Gibbs.

Lauren puts her arm around me and leads me out into the hall, "It is time for us to go now, this has been enough for one day." Ed agrees and we all leave.

Once in the car, Lauren starts talking endlessly almost nervously about nothing and anything. I am still reeling from the hypnoses. I have a nauseating headache, likening being poisoned.

I am in and out of sleep as Lauren drives me home. I am back in the blue azure water now and I am drowning. I open my eyes in my last seconds before I loose consciousness and become one with the water. After I acquiesce to the water, she bears her soul to me and now I know, somehow and in a real way Lauren, my best friend, was involved in these girls' murders. I see it.

The water envelopes me now, and as I am about to die, I then feel my father's arms around me lifeless, limp, little body and I know I will be ok. I leave my secrets in the blue azure water, they belong to her now. Lauren was involved.

And I let her majesty wash over me to forge what I have just learned and the grace to let it go.

"True friends are like stars. You don't always see them but you know they're always there."

"Immature love says, 'I love you because I need you.' Mature love says, 'I need you because I love you."

"Friends show their love in times of trouble, not in happiness."

""Good friends are hard to find, harder to leave, and impossible to forget."

Oh, Lauren!

The Devil

I can't breathe now, and I am suffocating, drowning in my own saliva. I am rustling with the Devil; he is front and center in my dream now and bearing down on me hard. "I got you now bitch, it is almost time, you are surrendering to me." "Anna, you are a liar of the deepest kind." "Souls like you are mine." "You keep sinister secrets."

"What do you want from me you vile beast?" He sonders back around me and curls up around me, squeezing me like a boa, "Everything," he answers. "Everything and then some." "I want your soul I want to burn you like white ashes, tortured from your separation from God." "I want it all, every bloody drop."

The devil wants you to profess your faith in Christ with your mouth, but for your actions to contradict Christianity. Nothing is more powerful than being a hypocrite. Even a lost and dying world despises hypocrisy. If the devil gets you confident enough of and in your faith to profess it, but weak enough in your faith to not follow it, he has created a powerful weapon for his plan.

The devil wants you to be afraid. The devil loves fear. Riots in the streets and economic uncertainty are breeding grounds for fear, anxiety, depression, and all other forms of human suffering and he delights in them all. Put the news on for five minutes and you will be convinced the world is falling apart, and do you know what, you wouldn't be wrong. When we are afraid, we just want to drown out the thing that is causing the fear. We want to numb the pain. Fear can be crippling. And when you focus on fear, he is winning.

The devil wants it all. He is greedy. He is selfish. Being a powerful angel in the Lord's presence wasn't enough for him. He wanted to be God. He will stop at nothing to take every good thing and destroy it. He is relentless and will go until he drains us of all of any good, we have, until we are hopeless and desperate and seek him out!

And with all of his proclamations, he simply says, "You belong to me, your souls are mine."

Bitter is the tarred
The bite just as marred
I will have you Anna!

CHAPTER SEVEN

The Police and I

I tell a good lie
I do it, so I can get by
You won't know the difference, you won't know the truth
You scandal and hide, you run aloof
The answers aren't out there
They belong with you

Even though I will never believe Victor killed Tiffany Garrett or Jenna Parker, Elise Frank's murder remains a quandary, Police believe that there is not enough evidence from my hypnosis to prove otherwise, at least we saved Karen Scott, I will always believe that we did! Victor was found guilty on the two capital murder charges and sentenced to death in Pennsylvania by lethal injection. I have decided to go and see Victor on death row and asked Office Pell, Jack, if he can get me in.

With Victor convicted now and the Eurotrash gone, the funerals for the dead girls over with, the Holly Oaks Country Club is getting back to normal. People are trying to move on. If Victor or the Eurotrash didn't kill these girls, who did? To everyone else, the world even, the killer is Victor, but I know better. There is a serial killer on the lose still in Farmington predating on innocent girls. I have tried to put all of this behind me now too, but I just can't. I feel like I may know something more, but it won't come forward and it won't come out. So, I decided to help in another way.

Office Pell and I have become friends and I have approached him about becoming a Police Officer full time. I will play tennis and even teach it from time to time, but my life has changed direction and course, this is where I want to be now, a State Trooper for the state of Connecticut. This whole experience has made me change the complete course of my life and I ended up here, wanting to be a police officer.

The Connecticut State Police is a division of the Connecticut Department of Emergency Services and Public Protection responsible for traffic regulation and law enforcement across the state of Connecticut, especially in areas not served by local police departments. Officer candidates must: Have a high school diploma or GED. Be at least 20 years of age. Be a US citizen. Have no felony, class A or B convictions. Be a resident of Connecticut and have a valid Connecticut driver's license before graduating from the training academy. I have already applied and been accepted and I will start at the Academy in two weeks. Office Pell and his wife Cindy ask me out for drinks to celebrate and I accept as long as it is anywhere but the Holly Oaks Country Club. He laughs and promises it will be a night to remember and a night never to forget!

I met Jack and Cindy at The Salt Air Restaurant in downtown Farmington close to the pavilion where they found Elise Frank's body. I am late so when I walk in, I can see the two of them already in a corner booth, but someone else is with them. They all three stand and Jack hugs me and Cindy does too, and then I turn and face this man, he must have been about 6'2 and lean, devastatingly handsome, my knees buckled and heart skipped a beat, "Hi", he says, "I am Ryan Murphy."

Ryan Murphy, I learned during dinner, is a detective and one hell of a tennis player. Ryan played tennis in college and was nationally ranked. There could not be any better two people to meet, so much in common and the instant attraction we both felt and it helped. Ryan took my number and promised he would call so that we could get together and play tennis and get to know one another better.

So, my life had changed course, but I was still me. I stopped giving lessons at the Club even though my knee has completely healed but I was still a member. I had to leave the Club in my past and when I am ready to give lessons again, it will be on my terms. I had to pay dues like everyone else now, and they were exorbitant. I liked it though, paying my way and using the Club the way I want to, when I want to. I have played a couple of sets with Eddie since coming back to the Club, he even beat me once. The Club is back into the swing of things since the arrest of Victor there seems to be some peace about it, that someone will pay for the deaths of Tiffany, Jenna, and Elise. In time, as time passes, the Club will move on to a new class of young debutants and beauty queens, but her walls and foundation will never forget what happened here. Their lives and deaths stain the windows and walls with transcendental memories, just like the memories of the 1950's when young couples came here to Jitterbug and Waltz, young lovers would sneak out back to the marina and fool around and the moon and stars would bear witness to it all. The inception of the Holly Oaks Country Club in 1954 will stay still in time like the erect little doll house with its perfect little furniture and perfect little life, secrets and lies, betrayal and murder. And that is way things just go in life, time moves on, people move on, but our memories make up the future.

My first date with Ryan was at the Club, but not to play tennis, just for cocktails and apps. He even picked my favorite appetizer, the Club's Calamari with Thai sauce. He was just too good looking and everyone agreed, men and women alike. He turned heads when he walked in a room----even children gawked. When Ryan entered the room, all took notice. After four drinks, two each, and the Calamari followed by two Cobb salads, we go for a drive. I show him Holly Oaks and we drive for miles and park at the 18th hole on the Fairway and hold hands. The sun is setting and over the fairway the green turf turns magenta and burnt orange as the Connecticut sun falls upon it. Almost too beautiful, frozen in time we are, between the red and orange hues.

Ryan reaches over and gives me our first kiss, riddled with passion, but solid with meaning. I ask him if he is up for another short drive, he says yes. The drive takes us only about ten minutes and then we are parked in my driveway facing my townhome. "Would you like to come in?" "It's pretty late Anna, don't you think." I appreciate his gentlemanly manners and his fake restraint, all part of his charm! "It is 8:30 Ryan.," I say. Just like that he follows me in the front door and up my stairs and lays down me on my own bed, the same bed where all my dreams happened, where the Devil came to visit, where the Witching Hours Lullaby sang to me. Things were different now, and I loved my bed and was filled with excitement over the new possibilities it would have for me. What happened next between Ryan and I was so needed by me, to feel a human presence that wasn't void or evil, to have Ryan inside of me, not invading me, rather knowing me, and loving me became my completion. These moments were not just sex, but euphoria down to my bare bones and nakedness. It was only then that I was able to really let go, and when I did, I came and at the same time let Ryan in forever.

He fell asleep in my arms but did wake and leave knowing I had an early morning. Today was the day----------------- I was driving to Pennsylvania to visit Victor on death row.

I have been prepped and read all of the instructions that I must follow while visiting the prison courtesy of Officer Pell.

Death row inmates are allowed up to three non-contact visits per week that are limited to one hour each while life without parole inmates may qualify for contact visits and are usually allowed at least two visits per week of at least one hour. Death-row prisoners are typically incarcerated in solitary confinement, subject to much more deprivation and harsher conditions than other prisoners. As a result, many experience declining mental health or try and commit suicide. It was your death before your death.

I stop for coffee on my way there at a 7eleven, but then drive straight through. I am panicked as my drive takes me closer and closer to the prison. The drive would take me four hours and I started losing breath in the last hour.

The Prison is massive and I enter in the side entrance three as I was instructed, once past security, I enter a long hallway and given a number like at a dry cleaner.

I wait. When I am called, I am shown to a small room with a table and two chairs and very bad lighting, resembling a hell hole. There was a mouse in the corner, it scurries across the floor. I swear in all of its scampering, it stops and looks me square in the eye.

The door opens and Victor enters handcuffed, shackled, and escorted by two security guards. His head down but looks up at me and our eyes meet and lock.

I stand up, "Hi, I am Anna Davis.," I offer a hand. He squints at me like a wounded animal, he looks so small, so fragile. "I remember you from the Holly Oaks Country Club, you re the tennis pro, right?" "Yes, I am Victor or I was." "Well, that doesn't matter, I am here to check on you, see how you are holding up?" "Holding up, are you kidding, I am rotting in here, I can't talk to my family back in Iceland and they are going to kill me for something I didn't do, I didn't do it, I didn't do it!" "I know you didn't kill Jenna Parker of Elise Frank; I know Victor, I am here as a friend." "Maybe I could contact your people in Iceland for you, or maybe even better get you access to a phone, I know people, people in high places, and I myself am going to be a Police Office in training." "I start the academy in two weeks." "From a tennis pro to a cop, WOW." "I want to help you Victor, what can you tell about me Tiffany Garrett?" "Why are you going out on a limb to help me, Anna?" "You don't even know me!" "I have been having dreams, wicked dreams and have been seeing a doctor for them and recently I was hypnotized." "I have seen visions of the girl's being murdered and know you didn't do it and I have told the Police everything." "Well, that did a lot of good didn't it," asks Victor? "Tell me about the night Tiffany dies, it may help, maybe I can relate to something, verify something, anything?" "Victor we must try."

"Tiffany, oh sweet Tiffany, I was falling in love with her." "I never wanted to hurt her, it just happened in the heat of passion, a tragic accident." He begun reciting the night Tiffany dies in dripping detail. He spoke of the group "Eurotrash that met up and formed at the Country Club kitchen, it consisted of five European young men who preyed upon women at the Club, trying to get a start at a life here in the States. The Club's focus was the "choking game, a sexual game of choking your lover almost to death." Cedric bowed out of the group almost immediately when his golden opportunity presented, that left Victor, Tom, Paul and Darrs. As Victor would tell it, Darrs just openly disappeared one day from the Club and never came back even leaving a paycheck behind? "It was rumored that he stole cash from the cash register." At that point Victor, Tom and Paul were left and starting honing in on three young rich girls, Tiffany, Jenna, and Elise. They secretly referred to the girls in private as the "Brat Pack." Tom and Paul paired off with Jenna and Elise, Victor, and Tiffany became close. He was happy, happier than even the times of his childhood in Iceland with family and friends. He is in America now and going to make it. He had a job, some money in his pocket and almost enough saved to get his own place, and he had Tiffany. Why would he blow it, the short answer, he didn't? He was finding his way when something went wrong, terribly wrong. "I am going to find a way out there to help you, Victor." "You have to do your part and keep up in here, be strong and I will be back."

I told him I would come back to visit after the Police Training, I would be gone for about a month and asked him if it was ok if I write, I promised to write to him. "I won't stop fighting for you and the truth Victor." Just like that I stand up and leave. I am back in my car now driving away from a Pennsylvania Prison into a Police Training Camp, from one extreme to the other, both in the name of justice.

The time is here, Andover, Connecticut is where I start training. I will actually be staying in a dorm type of situation with women half my age. Upon arrival, I got settled in my dorm quickly and thankfully only had to share it with two other women and they were indeed half my age; Rebecca is twenty-six and Dayna is twenty-seven. Our training was only two weeks, it consisted of obstacle courses, gun safety and training, simulations, classroom work and team skill building with bonding. A lot of the work that was required for graduation was done online prior to entering the Academy. The two weeks went by in the blink of an eye and I felt prepared, almost like a real cop.

Before graduation, I wrote Victor a letter, as promised. I told him I was graduating and would be coming to visit him again before I started my new duties as a Connecticut State Police Officer. I am still looking for any new evidence and seeking out the truth for you every day. I felt so empowered to become a cop, like destiny overload.

The day of graduation was filled with so much emotion for me, starting this wonderful new life as a Police Officer and being able to share it with Ryan and Jack Pell and his wife, even with Dayne and Rebecca and the great people I have met down here, but also filled with regret and hurt for the three girls lost, and my old life as a tennis pro. I missed Lauren and Eddie, (who were both invited, but couldn't make it), I even missed home. I missed my old life, but maybe I wasn't supposed to live that life I had settled into after all, maybe I was in that exact place at the right time, at the Country Club, knowing what I knew at that point in life so I could help with these murders and maybe, ultimately become a Police Officer. Maybe our lives do make sense after all if we choose to follow and believe in our path.

After graduation I drive home thinking about my life and the lives of those around me. I am thinking mostly about Victor and how the State of Pennsylvania has set the date for his execution in three short months. I found out this morning. I have to pull over on the shoulder of the road, I am having trouble breathing and once the car stopped, I vomited my anger out all over the road. I am sweating, I feel my heart pulsing and feel electric type vibrations on the left side of my body, I think I am going to have a heart attack, I think, I think, and then I pass out. I am back in the blue azure water, arms and legs flapping, my little mouth trying to scream for help, but no one is there, I simply stop breathing and go under.

I wake up just minutes later and start my car and drive fast down the road, pulling right in front of a car, almost colliding.

There just had to be a way to help Victor and I was going to find that way, come what may, whatever it takes. He is innocent man. He is an innocent man and he needs my help!

That's it, innocence, the Innocence Foundation, that is the answer.

The Innocence Foundation is organized as a non-profit consisting of conscientious persons who believe no one should serve prison time for a crime committed by someone else. They are dedicated to raising awareness in support of those who are and equipping their loved ones for the journey ahead.

They strive to meticulously research, document and convey facts concerning state agencies and their contributions to the solution – or problem – of wrongful convictions and avoidable prison deaths. They will coordinate with other like-minded non-profits, and they will report on specific innocence cases. Sometimes, they will be able to assist with forensic analysis of evidence or discovery. When able, they will refer you to outside persons or agencies equipped to address specific concerns.

They are not lawyers, so they do not give any legal advice nor or they partisan or political in anyway, but a great resource for Victor and if nothing else, a listening ear. I will call them tomorrow morning.

What are the 5 primary goals of the Innocence Project?

- Compensation. Exonerees are often freed after years of wrongful incarceration with few resources to help them rebuild their lives. ...
- Police Accountability. ...
- Prosecutorial Reform. ...
- Revealing Wrongful Conviction. ...
- Strengthening Forensic Science. ...
- Suspect Development and Investigation.

Causes of Wrongful Conviction

- Mistaken witness id. Eyewitness error is the single greatest cause of wrongful convictions nationwide, playing a role in 72% of convictions overturned through DNA testing. ...
- False Confession. ...

- False forensic evidence. …
- Perjury…
- Official misconduct.

Yes, I feel this is it, these are the people, and this is the organization that will prove Victor's innocence once and for all. That journey will begin tomorrow, for Victor, for me and for innocence.

As I pulled up in the driveway, I saw a Welcome Home Banner and Ryan standing outside with a large arm of roses, pink my favorite and now I am home, changed, but home. Ryan and I have been dating for a while now, and I feel like this is it again, I could be happy, we could be happy.

Ryan grabs me and kisses me softly and first then harder and pulls me inside. We make love for hours, then I fall asleep due to the love making combined with the long drive home. I awoke later and put on my silk robe and headed downstairs; the smell of the steps leads me into my kitchen where Ryan is cooking. "Well, that smells great, what have you got there?" "I bought some skirt steak at Trader Joe's and I decided to make a stir fry, I stopped at that little farmer's market on the corner you like and all veggies are super fresh." I pull my hair back and take a big whiff of the pot, "smells great, I can hardly wait."

"Hey hon, can you pour us a glass of wine," he asks? 'Sure, will do."

I walk over to the open wine bottle and pick up a wine glass but then notice something sparking in the bottom of the flute? I pull it out and it is unmistakably a gorgeous, brilliant, diamond ring, before I can turn around Ryan is on one knee and asks me to marry him.

I join him on the floor maybe because I was going to pass out myself, but there we were, together on my kitchen floor, a ring on my finger, glaring with pride, both so happy and in love, about to begin our future. Even though we had no idea what our future meant; two cops, one purpose, one soul.

CHAPTER EIGHT

Death Row

To lift my wings, but to fly
Seeks the air, but not the sky
A pale blue desolates
Will I try
To escape my torment
Before I die

I called Lauren first the next morning and told my best friend of my great news. We are planning a celebratory dinner this week. "I knew he would propose soon; I told you." says Lauren. "I can't wait to see you and do some bridal shopping, love you." she says.

My second call was to the Innocence Foundation and I have meetings set up Bettie Grimes, a seasoned case worker and she has been with the Foundation for twelve years. She has taught me the subtle differences between Corpus Delecti and the Quantum of Proof. She told me that it has always been the Prosecution's stance and position to always convict Victor. That is because Victor confessed to the murder of Tiffany Garrett, accidental or not, and there was evidence of DNA left on the mallet that killed Jenna Parker found hidden at the club, where he handled the knives and mallets many, many times, so it was not surprising to find his prints if the mallet had not been cleaned. The knife found in the lake had been dumped by the murderer after slashing Elise Frank's throat also had 2 DNA findings of Victor. The prosecution presented this case as a connect the dots murder conviction, the troubling part to Bettie and me and anyone with a brain in their head, was that there was nothing, not a shred of proof or evidence that linked Victor to Jenna Parker or Elise Frank, other than that he knew them and the DNA on the hammer and knife. There was no motive, no eye witness' and no proof, just circumstantial evidence.

The Police had him on the hook and the jury convicted for all three murders based on what the prosecution produced, there was an assumption of guilt that the prosecution laid upon that jury, that there was enough evidence to convict Victor for all three murders and further, the prosecution always brought up, if not him, who? The Quantum of Evidence was sufficient enough, the prosecution had met their burden. Victor was guilty.

Since Victor's highly publicized case was moved to Pennsylvania, because Connecticut didn't have the death penalty, media coverage was not that widespread here in Farmington. The prosecution got the death penalty and I thought that would help Victor case become more publicized, maybe even be grounds for an appeal. Victor's fire to burn out, he just faded away awaiting his life to end, just like so many other people's stories. The evidence was enough to have a jury connect their own dots and believe or make the presumption that Victor could have killed all three girls. It was plausible. His DNA was found all three murder weapons and he did already to confess to Tiffany's murder.

It was almost a given that Pennsylvania would give Victor the death penalty, it was a state with a rich history of executions, and Victor's case was no exception. The Governor was running for reelection and she wanted to appear tough on crime and be the first female Governor to sign the Death Penalty in the State of Pennsylvania.

Pennsylvania began carrying out executions in the early 1600s in the form of public hangings. In 1834, Pennsylvania became the first state in the U.S. to outlaw public executions and move the gallows to county prisons. In 1913, the state's capital punishment statute was amended to bring executions under the administration of the state rather than individual counties, and also changed the method of execution to electrocution. Between 1915 and 1962, there were 350 executions in Pennsylvania, including two women. The last prisoner executed by means of the electric chair was Elmo Smith in 1962. Pennsylvania passed a law in 1990 that changed the method of execution from electrocution to lethal injection, the current means of execution. Prior to 1976, Pennsylvania carried out 1,040 executions, the third highest number of any state. Only three executions have actually been carried out since reinstatement in 1976 despite the size of the state's death row, which for more than two decades was the fourth largest in the nation. The Commonwealth's death row has declined steadily in size from 246 in October 2001 to 175 in July 2016, without any executions, primarily as a result of death sentences being overturned in the courts and defendants being resentenced to life or less or acquitted. It is now the country's fifth largest death row.

Victor's trail moved fast and he awaits his sentence on death row by lethal injection. He is on suicide watch as nearly all inmates on death row are. He spends twenty-three hours in isolation in a 6x6 cell with no mattress, pillow, or blanket.

Victor's prison was in New Hope Pennsylvania right outside of Philadelphia. The drive was three and half hours-four hours, but I have made the drive once and I am going out again today. Ryan is coming with me, although reluctantly.

Jack had gotten a special pass for me, as I had asked him to, and I wanted to see Victor as much as I could before I couldn't anymore. I still couldn't wrap my head around the barbaric means of which they execute people in the United States, especially Pennsylvania, it was almost like next level torture with a peaceful ending.

In the United States, the typical lethal injection begins with the condemned person being strapped onto a gurney and given two intravenous cannulas ("IVs") are then inserted, one in each arm. Only one is necessary to carry out the execution; the other is reserved as a backup in the event the primary line fails. A line leading from The IV line in an adjacent room is attached to the prisoner's IV and secured so that the line does not snap during the injections.

The arm of the condemned person is swabbed with alcohol before the cannula is inserted. The needles and equipment used are sterilized. Questions have been raised about why these precautions against infection are performed despite the purpose of the injection being death. The several explanations include: cannulae are sterilized and have their quality heavily controlled during manufacture, so using sterile ones is a routine medical procedure. Secondly, the prisoner could receive stay of execution after the cannulae have been inserted. Third, use of unsterilized equipment would be a hazard to the prison personnel in case of an accidental needle stick.

Following connection of the lines, saline drips are started in both arms. This, too, is standard medical procedure: it must be ascertained that the IV lines are not blocked, ensuring the chemicals have not precipitated in the IV lines and blocked the needle, preventing the drugs from reaching the subject. A heart monitor is attached to the inmate.

In most states, the intravenous injection is a series of drugs given in a set sequence, designed to first induce unconsciousness followed by death through paralysis of the respiratory muscles and/or by cardiac arrest. The execution of the condemned in most states involves three separate injections (in sequential order):

Sodium Thiopental: is an ultrashort-action barbiturate, an anesthetic agent used at a high dose that renders the person unconscious in less than 30 seconds. Depression of respiratory activity is one of the characteristic actions of this drug. Consequently, the lethal-injection doses, as described in the Sodium Thiopental section below, will—even in the absence of the following two drugs—cause death due to lack of breathing, as happens with overdoses of opioids.

1. Pancuronium Bromide is a nondepolarizing muscle relaxant, which causes complete, fast, and sustained paralysis of the skeletal striated muscles, including the diaphragm and the rest of the respiratory muscles; this would eventually cause death by asphyxiation.
2. Potassium Chloride a potassium salt, which increases the blood and cardiac concentration to stop the heart via an abnormal heartbeat and thus cause death by cardiac arrest.

I am not sure if I believe in the death penalty, but where Victor is concerned, I AM NOT! Victor and I became friends. He also became friends with Ryan, Jack, and Bettie. Lauren even came to see Victor once with me but never returned, Victor had people who cared, even in the end. I did reach his mother and family in Iceland and was able to be a go between. I even arranged a phone call between him and his mother before he died, I did all I could, but it wasn't enough.

My dreamscapes and the places I have gone while I was sleeping and or in my sub conscience, shed some light on what happened here with these murders, but not sufficient. I often wonder why me? What did I have to do with all of this and why in the end I had come to love Victor? Victor was so brave and witty; I wish I could have known him in the real world instead of a tunneled-out death row prison living with the rats, the mice and the knowing of what was coming.

Victor

The night before my execution, I was able to call home to Iceland and speak with my whole family. None of my family wanted to come to my execution, it was just simply too painful for them. I only had ten minutes, but it was enough; love has no time limits and love has no boundaries, even in death. I thought the phone call went as well as it could, even though my poor mother broke down and my brother had to take the phone away from her. My mother spoke and then sang to me in Faroese, my favorite childhood song. Then like that the phone died on my end and the message played loudly your time is up. And quite literally, it was.

I lay on my slab now, (makeshift bed), and don't hear a peep, not even the guards coming by doing their rounds, keys jangling, and their boredom heard. The common routine of waiting and checking on those about to expire. Death Row is nothing if not, solitary in its confinement. When I am finally able to force myself to go to sleep, I begin to see it.

Something on the ceiling, like a red blot. My eyes come into focus, and the blot seems to be spilling across my ceiling, getting bigger and bigger until finally it starts to drip. The dripping turning into a sprinkle of blood splattering on the bed and myself as I jump up, "what the fuck?" My hands are covered in the blood.

Then it stops and the ceiling goes back to Ashen white the way it was prior, my hands are clean, I must be seeing things, I must be, I must be and then, it speaks. In a sinister way, both aghast and powerful, "Victor tomorrow you will be mine; your soul is mine to keep." Just then I knew it was Satan. "I prey on the weak and devour the hellish, and you little Icelandic boy will come to hell with me tomorrow." "I have your uncle's soul, he is here, he has been waiting for you." "Your uncle's friend is also here, but I banished him to the never-ending fire pit, where he will be tortured and suspended for the rest of his soulless being." "They left you when you needed them the most, bad men both of them, and if I get you that makes three."

I drop on my knees and immediately begin praying to God through Jesus 'name.

"I repent Satan, in the name of the Father, son and holy spirit." I chanted over and over and then suddenly he was gone. I feel peace and loved by God now-----knowing where I am headed with certainty.

The mouse is back in the corner of my cell, and I am sure he heard everything. My eyes are heavy and fade to black as there is now humming all around me, a sweet lullaby being sung to me by mother and I am ok, the Witching Hours Lullaby lulls me to sleep on the eve of my death.

I am about to fall and asleep and right before I enter my last sleep alive, I see God appear before me, as quiet as a mouse and enormous in stature, he says "Welcome home Angel."

The mouse that was in my cell was now lying next to me right, by my ear and I didn't mind. I fall asleep with my mouse, the last loving creature that came to me, with no fear of what tomorrow will bring.

The night it happened, and Victor left this world, the guards that had been by Victor's side the whole time he was on death row, (two years and seven months), had become his friends and family. Walter David and Kenneth Hobbs walked Victor to the room where he would be executed. The long walk down the corridor to where Victor would meet his death.

At the end of their walk all three men stood outside of the cold, sterile room filled with three more people, the man who would start the execution and turn on the switch, the Warden, and another guard. Walter and Kenneth both hugged Victor and were both crying and as Kenneth let go, Victor slipped a letter into his hand. The Warden led Victor into the room, Victor looked back and mouthed the words "letter," give the letter to Anna Davis. Victor then looked straight ahead and entered the cold, grey room without any more fear or anything left but love.

Once strapped into the gurney, Victor is hoisted up so high he could see down below. Once in the air, the gurney spins around so that he is facing a wall with a curtain over it, like an old-fashioned movie screen. When the curtain opened, Victor could see about fifteen people sitting in front of him all in chairs like a baseball game, staggered in fear and resentment.

Amongst the people there to witness his execution were Tiffany's parents, Jenna's family, and Elise's parents and then he looked to the left there sat Anna Davis.

Anna mouthed the words, love.

"Do you have any final words to say," asked the stern guard, "Now would be the time." "I am innocent." Those were Victor's last words and then, **it is over.**

CHAPTER NINE

Dream again

To dream again
My little child
To feel love again
Soft and mild
Safe and secure, you never were
What just happened was all a blur

After Victor's execution Ryan and I took a short trip to Reykjavik to visit Victor's family and take his ashes to them. I paid to have Victor cremated and kept his ashes with me until Ryan and I could take the time and make this trip. I felt I owed it to Victor in part, but mostly because I am a Cop and this journey I have made began with Victor and ended with him too. Ryan and I were only in Iceland three days, but from Connecticut the flight was only five hours. So, the trip wasn't that taxing, after meeting his parents, brothers, and sisters, I knew being a Cop and working with the Innocence Foundation was my path and with Ryan by my side the whole time I knew I wouldn't have to do this alone. At the end of our trip his mother pulled me aside and whispered in my ear the words I will never forget, the words that define me as a human, as a Cop, as Victor's friend, for me; she said softly; tah-k and bles-h, thank you and goodbye.

Once settled back home I met Lauren for lunch and catch up. She has been busy working and focusing on her marriage and being my friend. Lauren was there for me in the beginning and all the way through, a great friend, we are even closer now. We met for lunch at Jimmy's Famous Seafood downtown. Our tradition when we come here is to always order a seafood Bloody Mary, garnished with shrimp and a crab legs. When she just orders an iced tea, I grab her hand and ask her if she I ok? She told me she is getting ready to turn forty-nine and just found out she is pregnant. "Look at me almost fifty and pregnant for the first time." "Al finally spent some time at home and look what happens!" We hug in the booth and laugh and cry. "I am going to be Auntie." This confirms to me that life can move on in even under the most heavy and difficult times. "Yes, a baby for me and a wedding for you," she says. We just held each other and in that moment with the smell of seafood in the air at Jimmy's,' we were more than ok!

My knee is better than ever and Ryan and I have been giving it a great workout playing tennis together, it seems when we are not working this is where we are, tearing up the turf! The Club has changed so much, but we have decided to try and revive it. If we made it through, others may too.

I do miss Eddie and things the way they were before it all happened. He left the Club and retired to parts unknown, just to have a quiet life and find peace, I guess. I got a letter from him about a month ago, with no post mark. I found that strange, but Eddie was never what you would call, "normal." The letter was very brief, but he asked me how his beloved Crepe Myrtles were doing? Ryan and I are BFFs with Jack Pell and his wife and they just adopted a dog, Ginger, and we are always pet sitting and completely in with her, Ryan has brought up adopting too and I say, "Let's get the wedding done with then we can think about it."

The Club has made many changes too. The kitchen has a whole new staff and there are new faces everywhere at the Club. There are faces that will never be forgotten. In the hallway before you enter the grand ballroom, the Club put up their pictures in gold frames, one of Tiffany, one of Jenna and one of Elise, never forgotten, here or anywhere, always in our hearts.

It has been almost three years since the murders and Farmington and Holly Oaks are both beginning to heal even though the real killer was never found. Many believe Victor was justly punished and executed, Tiffany and Jenna's parents, while others continue to search for the truth including Elise's family.

I stay in touch with the Frank Family and they have become involved with and donate to the Innocence Foundation, always searching, doing, and never giving up, holding out for their truth.

As for me, I am exactly where I want to be, a Cop, a Fiancée,' a friend, an Auntie, and one hell of a tennis player!

I sleep well now and there are no more bad dreams, break throughs or dreamscapes, and the Devil has finally left me alone, I am starting to think I actually made it through. The Witching Hours Lullaby does not sing her song to me anymore.

The days and nights of being laid up after surgery with my knee on OxyContin have faded, just a distant memory. But it did happen to me, and I take with me the experience of what I have learned into my bright and happy future:

The Innocence Foundation got some really bright light shone upon them during Victor's battle and they were all just angels, being called to do what they do. According to the **Innocence** Foundation it is estimated, between 2.3 percent and 5 percent of all US **prisoners** are **innocent.** I learned through my process. The judicial system is not perfect, not even fair that is why I decided to become a Cop and pursue justice and equality for all. It is a matter of grave importance.

I do not believe everyone person gets the same chance at life, love, justice, that good things happen to bad people and bad things happen to good people all of the time even in death.

Mysterious always, understood; rarely.

We can't say with certainty that we can fight this injustice and win, but we have to keep on trying for everyone's sake.

I believe in dreams and that somewhere between reality and dreamscapes maybe that is where the truth is really lurking waiting to be dug out like a rare pearl in a clam.

I was chosen, it was me. I am the pearl in that clam. I was put on this path and I was able to help save Karen Scott's life and I am so grateful to have known Victor even for as briefly as I did. I was sent for Victor, I think I may have been his Guardian Angel and he mine, I miss him more than words can say and grieve in my heart so heavy, that sometimes it is hard to breathe. People come into our lives and leave our lives; some stay always in our life even after death.

The wind now blows around me with remembrance, not the same, just different.

I am back in the blue azure water, the same water I nearly drowned in when I was six years old. Breathing is wrenching and I am dying. The blue azure water symbolic; trying to show me the way, my way. Bubbles come up to the surface as I go under and my breathing stops. I need to break the surface, I need to be clear.

I also believe in the Devil, as it has come to be. He has revealed himself to me and shown me such wicked things, things people do not ever want to know. I truly believe he is gone now, and so is my journey. I am here, living and breathing and ready to begin again.

And this is life; all these things, the little things, the big things, the salubrious ardor we all strive for. You, me; here.

Myopic in our judgments, but desperate to be here.

CHAPTER TEN

The Witching Hours

Darkness is here
For me and You
No strength here to get us through
You die, I live, right on cue
This meaningless wretch leaves us a morning dew

The Devil came to me one final time. It was during broad daylight when I was at the Harris Teeter Grocery Store in Holly Oaks. I couldn't see the beast, as I had before, but knew it was there. When I rounded the frozen food aisle I smelled a foul distinctive smell, like rotting garbage or a rotten corpse and then I saw the door fly open where the frozen waffles and breakfast meats were. He was there, challenging me, one last standoff. The cold hit me and shivers ran down my spine right before the Devil himself said you win, and in a nano second it was like nothing had ever happened, he just simply went away! I walk down the frozen food aisle and pushed my cart to the cashier, next in line.

The Witching Hour is the time of day when humanity has the potential to become more aware of the activity happening beyond the veil, in the spiritual realm. While the name implies it's a specific hour... It's actually the period of time between the end of the night, and the beginning of a new day. In the Western Christian tradition, the hour between 3 and 4 a.m. was considered a period of peak supernatural activity – this time is also referred to as the "Devil's hour" due to it being a mocking inversion of the time in which Jesus supposedly died, which was at 3 pm.

The witching hour may stem to a human sleep cycle and circadian rhythm--- the body is going through REM sleep at that time, which is the deepest sleep, where the heart rate is lower and the body temperature reduced and breathing pattern and blood pressure is irregular. Therefore, sudden awakening from the deepest sleep would cause agitation, fear, and disorientation to an individual. Also, during REM sleep, which usually occurs within the witching hour, unpleasant and frightful sleep disturbances such as parasomnias can be experienced, which include nightmares, REM sleep, behavioral disorders, night terrors and sweats, sleepwalking, homicidal sleepwalking, and sleep paralysis.

Moreover, during the night and well into the witching hour, symptoms of illnesses and condition such as heart disease, asthma, and flu-like symptoms even the common cold seem to exacerbate because there is less cortisol in the blood late at night and especially during sleep. As such, the immune system is very active and white blood cells that fight infections in the body during sleep, and this would thereby worsen the symptoms even nasal congestion, cough, fever, chills, and sweating.

The Witching Hours held me captive for so long, they were where my dreams took place and where these lives were exposed to me, both the living and the dead. I will never forget this experience and hold this special to my heart, as it was I who helped the Police, it was why I became a Cop and it was I, who lived through this.

I met the devil during my Witching Hours, but he is gone now forever and this I know is true. I moved on from him and everything that he represents. But I am glad I met him once upon a time because I faced my fears and bad decisions there with him and was able to leave that all behind and move forward and create a healthy life void of his existence.

I denounce the devil and have accepted the peace of Jesus Christ in my heart, and I forever will ride high, and be safe now and forever!

The Witching Hours swoop down upon me, But I am gone now, no more Anna for them to feast on!

The Devil

To some, simply put, the Devil does not exist. To others, especially Christians, their faith is that you can't believe in God and not believe in Satan, you can't have the goodness without the evil. Some just accept Satan as the cartoon character with pointy horns and a red face and long tail, not ever knowing his power and ability to demise. To others Satan can be a lover, an antichrist or even possessions luring down unpaved, dark roads.

Satan and his demonic forces incite spiritual warfare and all forms of opposition to God's work of salvation, God's people, and the mission of the Church on earth. And to steal, kill and destroy. Jesus has said through John 10:10 – "The thief comes only to steal and kill and destroy; I have come that they may have life and have it to the full."

So, it seems that the devil enjoys the feeling of power and having power over someone—and he gets great pleasure in controlling us, in making us his subjects, and even in making and seeing us suffer. He wants to destroy us, and he wants us to suffer until to its bitter end, he has us right where he wants us far apart from God.

Eternal separation from God is what hell really is. How he destroys you here on this Earth and takes your soul into the next is by bearing false witness to you about better things and then lying and cheating you, this makes you want those things even more and you turn to hm for those things.

The devil's last words to me were lingering like a bad metaphor or a damning wish. "I go now, but not in peace my dear Anna, I have used you as long as I can now." "But always remember, I was here and showed you many wicked things and made you to suffer like they did, you can't erase your own pain or deny I brought it upon you."

"They are dead, and I lust for their souls, but they are not mine to take." "You my dear, are the one that I want, not good, not bad, just stumbling around in this world oblivious of what is yet to come." "It may not be soon, but inevitably, I feel, you and I will meet again and until that time has come, I leave Victor's death on you and the unsolved murders to haunt your dreams." "I leave you no peace with their blood on your hands." "You kept the secret about Lauren and did not pursue it, you caused death, you did this."

"I will be back to run this earth in the final days when the ground is mine and the earth rots at her core, every living soul will have to take my number 666, all will bow to me." "I will be omnipotent and in charge of all that are left behind because you poor souls will be all mine, and when that time has come, I will be looking for you."

Until then...................

Blue Azure Water

When I was six years old, I was on a boat with my family celebrating something, but I was too young to remember. Everyone was happy though, laughing and living, I think it was someone's birthday.

All I do remember is, in one second eating Doritos out of a red bag, to the next being thrown over the back of the boat.

I flew off the back of the boat, quickly, like a bird with no wings.

It took a full minute for anyone to realize what had happened. It was the longest sixty seconds for me. When I hit the water, my little legs and arms betrayed me, and I immediately began to sink. All my energy left me, and I became weightless, maybe like a mermaid. *The blue, azure water calms me, easing the burning of my lungs and the pain in my body.*

It was in the last five seconds before I stopped breathing that I opened my eyes and fell in love with the water; she was mysterious, yet familiar and beckoned me home. Then there was nothing left of me, I became one with the water.

And then finally, I stopped fighting and let go. The letting go freed me and all the fear left my little being, and I was ok to drown.

It was in letting go that I became free; a mermaid, a sea creature, me!

Seconds later I felt the pressure of my dad's arms around my small, limp body and somehow, in that moment, I knew that I would be ok.

The Blue Azure water shared by Anna, Eddie, and Victor.

EPILOGUE

....

Life and death go hand and hand
Around the beaten bush
No one knows when or how
A glimpse, a shove, a push
It comes to meet with violent dread
The morning of a dead man's thread
Unspools itself unworthy
Rotten flesh following where it becomes dirty

I heard through the grapevine that Karen Scott got married to an investment banker out of New York City and his net worth is said to be around 200 million, a man named Jason Wentworth, a big-time stock analyst featured in Forbes and Time Magazine. The word at the Country Club is that she moved to the Upper East Side and was living the good life, happy, free, and alive; a victim's victim she was not! A mother to two girls and an activist for the ACLU, working pro bono and spending any free time she has working for the Innocence Fund. A trophy wife, she had not become!

I miss Eddie, he left Holly Oaks last year and I have lost touch with him, as people do from time to time. He just left no forwarding address. My only thoughts of Eddie now are that somehow, he found what he was looking for. I had come to know that Eddie had not had an easy life, the death of his father and when he and his mother made it to the United States, her whole life had to work at least two jobs to support herself and Eddie. After she died young, she left Eddie alone just a young man in this big world, I loved Eddie and I feel that he would be ok, that this world owed him something, something real, something good.

The last time I saw him he simply said wished me luck and left in a hurry, said he was looking for somewhere new to live his golden years, needed a fresh start. "Take care of my babies----those vivid pink crepe myrtles, his trees, his babies." Eddie said he felt sadness for Victor after the execution, and he knew he was innocent--- the way he said those words to me gave way to chills down my spine although I never understood why. His eyes were cold that day, defunct and departed. Like he was trying to tell me something, and I could not hear him. Look deeper Anna, look in between that where the truth is hidden. Our souls connected by it, imparted like a valiant prize, unworthy of knowing you and unfeeling in my departure. Goodbye Anna.

Victor would have been released from Prison on December 30th, 2029, if the punishment actually fit the crime. If he were just charged with unvoluntary manslaughter for the death of Tiffany Garrett, he would have been a free man today. Right in time for the lunar eclipse which is between December 20 – 31, 2029, the second of two Metonic twin eclipses, will occur. The first of the twin eclipse pair happened from December 21 to 22 in 2010. Once every nineteen years something so special on this Earth.

Like the lunar eclipses, Victor's life was lived upside down. A victim first, a scared kid second, and everything else he became triturated and manducated. His life but a fleeting laser of light, just like the dramatic total eclipse which will plunge the full moon into deep darkness as it passes right through the center of the Earth's umbral shadow. A spectacular gift while here.

Three young girls are now dead, and we do not know who killed the last two. We only know that it was indeed Victor who killed the first girl, Tiffany Garrett eight years ago, but was meant to pay the price in his blood.

The DNA evidence introduced in the trial three months before his execution proved that someone else's semen was on the third victim's panties, Elise Frank. It was not the DNA evidence belonging to Victor Guðmundsdóttirr on that crime scene nor was there enough evidence to tie him to the second or third crime scene. He was only truly found guilty of killing Tiffany Garrett in the heat of the moment that awful night, maybe had he been tried for that crime alone, he may have been spared his life. If things weren't covered up in this trial, or put on such a stall, things could have moved faster and proven Victor's innocence. If this evidence had been brought to light and reviewed quicker, Victor may be alive today.

Our justice system is not perfect, but actually broken into a million little pieces with a few honest people trying to fix it and put it back together again and make it whole. The business of savings lives, not taking them.

Life is sometimes a puzzle and sometimes people just want a finished picture—a beautiful image, so they force the pieces in where they do not belong. Maybe they do this because they do not want to do the work, or they are depressed, in grief, oblivious, or just don't care, but you have to have your pieces sorted before you can place them, this shouldn't be daunting, but exciting. That puzzle is our lives, our collective lives, you, and me together and we must pay attention and help one another because when this happens the puzzle comes together and we all win.

I fought for him, his life, my life, life in general for the people.

I do this because I am Cop, a Police Officer, and this is what we do protect and serve.

The year Victor would have been released in 2029 would have been met with challenges; Donald Trump died in June after choking on a Bic Mac, we have our first female president, Elizabeth Warren, you can only use Bitcoin to buy things, everyone drives an electric car and you watch movies at home, movie theaters are extinct., but Victor was executed a life sacrificed for the unjust!

But it is only 2024 and I just turned fifty-four. I am married now to fellow Police

Officer, Ryan Murphy and happy. Finally, a good man I have and cherish and he plays a mean game of tennis. Tennis is where it began and continues with me now.

I was recently promoted to Captain of my Police Department at the State Level in Connecticut, from a tennis instructor to Police Captain, what a road I have hoed. I have become a different person and I like me; I love me.

Lauren's baby Aiden is now one year old and a handful, but her little family is so beautiful and we are all so close, Familia.

The three girls that were murdered in Farmington Connecticut in 2021 will never leave me, their faces, their families, their lives, their deaths. I am a Cop and as a good cop, their stories became my story. They are part of me now and I carry them with me behind my badge next to my heart.

Ryan and my Police Department are working to create a new way of looking at forensic evidence and DNA before a trial actually begins. So that when you are in the middle of a trial with someone's life or death on the line, you already know what the DNA will prove or won't prove. Hopefully, quelling convictions of the unjustly accused and narrowing the path to finding a more direct route for the guilty, shedding light to the Innocence Fund.

Ryan and I went out and celebrate my promotion at Artie's by the water. Holding hands and smooching behind folded menus, sipping champagne, and saying I love you under every breath. By the time our cheesecake was served I was completely convinced that he was the one for me forever, I finally found my home.

Ryan leaves Artie's and heads to my place, I tell him I need to stop at the station and pick up some reports, but I promised not to take too long. "I will keep the bed warm," he says, as I pull away and head out into the rain. I knew there was weather coming and I had planned to work from home tomorrow and needed these files.

The cold December rain is falling hard and turning quickly to sleet, I must get these reports and get home quickly. These Connecticut storms can blow up fast, so I have learned.

Once inside the station, I head to my office and retrieve my needed reports from the file cabinet. I am about to leave, but as I turn, I notice a piece of mail on my desk, a card. I reached for it, clutch in my right hand, and knew immediately it was from Victor. Where did this come from and how did it get here? I look over my shoulder, but only the dark hallways are there, quiet as a mouse.

I don't wait, I open the card immediately, in terror, in anguish, in relief, in love.

The card was signed Love, Victor and on the card was a shorthand written letter to me.

Dear Anna,

It is the eve of my execution, and I am sitting here thinking about what will come next for me.

Thanks to you and the time we have spent with Father McLean I know I will go to Heaven because Jesus has forgiven my sins. I am not afraid to die, but more afraid of not being able to live and not being able to live a full, healthy, truthful life, but I can now in this moment, in my final moments.

I did not kill Jenna Parker or Elise Frank. I do admit to killing Tiffany Garrett and I have repented for it. I am not even sure how it all happened that night, why I did it, I do not even understand myself, but I did it and I am sorry. I forgave myself a long time ago and believe me on Death Row you have nothing but time and alone time with your thoughts, maybe that is the purpose of death row, your final repentance.

I love you Anna and I thank you. Tell my family in Iceland how much I love them too and maybe one day you will make it out there, to my island, that is my final wish that you go to Iceland and see the treasures it offers; from the Blue Lagoon, to the Glaciers, Geysers and Volcanos, and how I love that this is my final wish for you, ég elska þig, I love you Iceland!

And finally, I leave with you my last confession as I do not want to take it with me after death, I leave it here with you, to take care of it, as I know you will.

Throughout my time on death row, I confessed this knowing to my two friends the Guards, who will be with me at my execution, but no one would listen to a convicted murderer from Iceland sitting on death row. Even those who came to love me in here and became my family, they didn't believe me, but I knew you would, so to you, I say.

I met him only briefly at the Club, he was fiddling with the big Crepe Myrtle Trees, called him his babies. He was a groundkeeper; I think or a landscaper? He had a dirt on him, seen and unseen. He had eyes of ember and a stare of viciousness. He was void, on the hunt. He was not a human or a person, but a thing. He killed those girls at the Country Club and mutilated their bodies, he bragged about to me and the Eurotrash Group. He wanted to the big man at the Country Club. He wanted the chance he never had to be famous for something, known for anything. He burned one girl in an abandon barn after bludgeoning her to death, and the other he disposed of at the wharf near the American Marina somewhere in the woods after he slashed her throat. Maybe remnants can be found, maybe you can head this search.

One more thing though, he said he had an accomplice-a woman that was all he ever said about her other than that she was motivated by hate, she hated those girls too. Reminiscent of a life she lost, a life she couldn't have back or one she never had at all.

As for me, I will be injected with chemicals and poisons that will stop my breathing and my heart tomorrow and I will be gone. No more me, no more Victor.

I didn't kill those girls. Keep me with you Anna.

Good people are always immortal, carry me with you in your fight for justice.

Always,
Victor
P.S. And the killer is………………………………

Keep dreaming, keep following your instincts, keep on believing in yourself! You and you alone determine your worth and write your own story, you are brave, you are worthy, you are you. Lastly, to all the dreamers who dare to dream even through the witching hours. You are heard through music, through vibrations, through words, through the whispers that scare us all.

To Christopher, Caroline, Stacie, Mom, and Brad of course Lu!

With special thanks to the Devil himself, for showing me real evil, without it, I couldn't know the path of Jesus and all that is good.

Evil and good rival one another, one can't exist without the other, for this is the purpose of our soul.

For God so loved the world that he gave his only begotten son, whosoever believe in him shall not perish but have life eternal.

Shannon Gill Burnett

To all the late bloomers and those who think they are too old,
or their chances have passed them by
Remember it is never too late
I am a late bloomer; I didn't receive my first kiss until I was 18, I didn't get
my driver's license until I was 19 and I didn't have a boyfriend until I was 20
I didn't start living a true life until I was 33, when I
understood what it meant to serve people
AND... I didn't become a woman until this moment
where I can say, I have fully arrived.
My late father called me a diamond in the rough, well Daddy, I
am no longer your diamond in the rough, I am the Diamond!

The End

ABOUT THE AUTHOR

....

Shannon Gill Burnett author of *In the Medium* published by iUniverse 2012. This is her second book published with us.

Printed in the United States
by Baker & Taylor Publisher Services